'A ten-rounder!' Pop Mauler said. 'The Fonz versus The Muskogee Mauler!'

The crowd began cheering again.

'Hold it!' Fonzie protested.

'With a prize of a hundred dollars to the winner!' Pop Mauler announced.

'Don't hold it!' Fonzie said.

'And I personally will handle all bets that the local citizens want to place on the hero of the hour – The Fonz!' Pop Mauler told the crowd.

People began reaching for their wallets.

'The fight of the century will be held on the final night of the carnival . . .'

Also in *Tandem*

HAPPY DAYS 2 : THE BIKE TYCOON

HAPPY DAYS 1
THE FONZ AND LAZONGA

William Johnston

A TANDEM BOOK
published by
TANDEM PUBLISHING Ltd

A Tandem Book
Published in 1977
by Tandem Publishing Ltd
A Howard and Wyndham Company
44 Hill Street, London WIX 8LB

Printed in Great Britain by
Hazell Watson & Viney Ltd, Aylesbury, Bucks

ISBN 0 426 18374 6

ONE

Standing at the edge of a large open space at the edge of town, Richie Cunningham and his two friends Potsie and Ralph, watched the arrival of the Hagle Bros. Carnival. It was early morning, only a few hours after sun-up, and the boys were still somewhat sleepy-eyed. But they were excited, too. Because for weeks the posters that had heralded the arrival of the carnival had been promising: Thrills! Rides! Girls!

With amazing efficiency, the roustabouts began unloading the equipment from the trucks and erecting the rides and putting up the tents that would hold the sideshows. They worked as if they were fitting together the pieces of a jigsaw puzzle that they had completed so many times before that they could now do it from memory—possibly even with their eyes closed.

"I bet they'll have the whole thing up by noon," Ralph said, awed.

Potsie pointed to where a gang of roustabouts was unloading wide seats and latticelike sections of steel framework. "That's going to be the Ferris wheel!" he said.

"It's the biggest Ferris wheel in the world!" Ralph said.

"Every carnival has the biggest Ferris wheel in the world," Richie said. "But they all look the same size to me."

They turned their attention to the far side of the lot, where the tents for the sideshow were going up.

"JoJo The Dog-Faced Boy," Ralph said, reading from a large canvas that the workers had spread out on the ground. "What kind of a dog does he have a face like, I wonder."

"A bulldog," Potsie said. "Big deal. A lot of guys have a face like a bulldog. Now, if he had a face like a collie, that would be something."

"He could be a movie star," Ralph said.

"Who'd want to see a movie star with a face like a collie?" Richie asked.

"It hasn't hurt Lassie," Ralph replied.

"The Muskogee Mauler," Richie said, reading, as another canvas was spread out on the ground. "He must be the prize fighter."

"That, I want to see—a real professional fighter," Potsie said. "Have you ever seen one of those carnival fighters? They've got muscles on their muscles!"

"Can't you win some money by going a couple rounds with those guys?" Richie asked.

"That's what they tell you," Ralph said. "But have you ever seen it happen? You step in the ring, and pop, thats' it—you're out."

"No, I saw it happen once," Potsie said. "Some guy from town here stayed a whole three rounds with one of those guys. It was a couple years ago. I was a kid then."

"Once in a hundred years," Ralph said.

"Hey!" Potsie whooped, pointing.

The workmen were raising the canvas for the Isles of Paradise. Painted on it were the figures of a number of shapely young women in grass skirts. They appeared to be performing a hula.

"Hoochie-coochie dancers!" Ralph said, bug-eyed.

"I know a guy who dated a hoochie-coochie dancer once when a carnival was in town," Potsie said.

"What happened?" Richie asked.

"What do you think happened?"

"I don't know—what happened?"

"Listen, what do you expect to happen when you date a hoochie-coochie dancer?" Potsie countered.

"Did it?" Ralph asked.

"All I know is, the guy lost his wallet," Potsie replied.

"What's that supposed to mean?" Richie asked.

"If he lost his wallet, something was going on, wasn't it?" Potsie answered.

"Maybe she just picked his pocket," Ralph said.

"If she did, it was because she got close enough to," Potsie countered. "And if she got *that* close, there was something more than pocket-picking going on."

"I don't know," Ralph said, unconvinced. "Where was he carrying his wallet? If it was in his hip pocket, she could have sneaked up behind him and never even touched him."

"When you date a hoochie-coochie dancer, you don't stand around with your back to her," Potsie said.

"What do you do?"

"What do you think you do when you date a hoochie-coochie dancer?"

"Did they?" Richie asked.

Potsie looked at him puzzledly. "Did who?"

"This guy you know and the hoochie-coochie dancer."

"He lost his wallet, didn't he?" Potsie answered. "*Something* must have been going on."

"Madame LaZonga," Ralph said. "What does she do?"

Richie and Potsie returned their attention to the sideshow area, where another canvas was being raised. It depicted a gypsy woman gazing raptly into a crystal ball.

"She's the fortune teller," Richie said. "My mother had her fortune told once. A gypsy was going from door to door with her own teapot and tea leaves and everything."

"What did she tell her?" Potsie asked.

"She told her she was going to meet a stranger who would have news for her."

"Wow!" Ralph said. "Did it happen?"

Richie nodded. "We got a new paperboy," he said.

"There goes the caterpillar," Potsie said, pointing to where the rides were being erected. "I used to be scared of that when I was a kid. I was afraid of the dark."

"I used to be afraid of the dark, too," Ralph said. "I got over it by closing my eyes."

Richie and Potsie peered at him.

"Closing your eyes?" Richie asked.

"So I couldn't see that it was dark," Ralph explained.

From the distance came the low guttural growl of a motorcycle engine.

Turning, Richie, Potsie and Ralph saw a large red

bus approaching the carnival grounds, preceded by Fonzie on his bike.

"Why is that bus chasing The Fonz?" Potsie asked curiously.

"No, I think he's leading it," Richie said. "It must be lost."

"Why is he bringing it here?" Ralph wondered.

"Maybe he has a job steering customers to the carnival," Potsie guessed.

"Hey! It's the carnival bus!" Richie said.

"Look at all those girls!" Ralph said. "They must be the hoochie-coochie dancers!"

"That explains it," Potsie said. "The Fonz is always one step ahead of everybody else. He must have met the bus at the city line and dated up all the hoochie-coochie dancers."

"We better warn him to keep one hand on his wallet," Ralph said.

Fonzie pulled up where Richie, Ralph and Potsie were standing and switched off his motor. The bus halted, too.

"Thanks for the help!" the driver called down to Fonzie.

"Hey! It was my civic duty!" Fonzie replied. "I couldn't leave the hoochies and the coochies stranded, could I? The town nerds would never forgive me."

The girls, laughing and giggling, began calling down to Fonzie.

"I'm Tuesday afternoon, don't forget!" a blonde said.

"Normally, that's when I do my ironing," Fonzie replied. "But this week I'll go wrinkled."

"I'm Wednesday night!" a redhead called out.

"Don't forget me—I'm Thursday night!" a dark-haired girl reminded Fonzie.

"Hey! Hey! Hey! Keep your grass skirts on!" Fonzie said. "You girls got to do your own remembering, who is who and when is when. You do the remembering and The Fronz will do his part—by showing up.

The girls cheered.

Fonzie motioned to the driver. "Thataway!" he said, pointing toward the carnival grounds.

The bus moved on, with the hoochie-coochie dancers leaning out the windows waving and blowing kisses to Fonzie.

Richie, Ralph and Potsie stared at Fonzie in open-mouthed wonder.

"What's the matter?" he asked, looking at himself, "did I put my body backwards in my clothes or something this morning?"

"Those girls!" Richie said, recovering somewhat.

"Yeah, that's what those are," Fonzie responded, looking after the bus. "You're growing up, Cunningham. You don't have to have pictures drawed for you any more."

"You're dating them?" Ralph said. "*All* of them?"

"As many as I can," Fonzie replied. "It depends on how long the carnival is in town. I got afternoons and nights booked up. But if dating them all means that I have to give up my mornings too, then some of them are gonna miss out—a hoochie here and a coochie there. A man's got to keep his mornings free for his personal whatchamacallits."

"His personal whats?" Ralph asked.

"I got to brush my teeth, don't I? I got to wash my socks, don't I?"

"How did you meet them, Fonz?" Richie asked.

"You heard about the fickle finger of fate?"

Richie nodded.

"Well, The Fonz's finger of fate is true blue," Fonzie told him. "It knows if it's ever fickle to The Fonz, it'll get a rap right in the mouth. That's how I met them."

"Could you go into a little more detail?" Richie asked.

"When I left the house this morning on my bike," Fonzie said, "my finger of fate pointed down this street that I never go down. I never go down it because if I did, it would take me out of my way. But, this morning, this finger pokes itself in my back and says, 'This is a stickup! Go down this street that you never go down or I'll shoot!'" He shrugged. "What could I do?"

"And so?" Potsie said.

"So, I go down this street," Fonzie replied. "And there is this bus with all these hoochie-coochies aboard. The bus is stopped and the driver has the hood up."

"Engine trouble!" Ralph said.

"No, eye trouble," Fonzie responded.

"He lost his glasses under the hood," Ralph guessed.

"No, the distributor cap was off, only the driver, with his eye trouble, couldn't see it," Fonzie said.

"So you fixed it," Potsie said.

"Hey, hold it!" Fronzie said. "What am I, a nerd? What do I do, come upon a busload of hoochie-coochies with the distributor cap off, and I fix it and send them on their way, presto chango?"

"What *did* you do?" Richie asked.

"I looked for the trouble," Fonzie replied. "I kicked

the tires—that wasn't the trouble. I rubbed some of
the grime off the back window—that wasn't the trouble. And, while I'm looking for the trouble, I am also
passing the time of day with the hoochie-coochies.
We got to know each other. Naturally, by the time I
got around to discovering that the distributor cap was
off, they was trying to date me up. They may be
beautiful, but they're not dumb." He looked toward
the sideshow area. "Madame LaZonga," he said. "She
was on the bus, too. Her and her daughter."

"Did she tell your fortune?" Potsie asked.

"When those hoochie-coochies started dating me
up, nobody *had* to tell my fortune," Fonzie replied.
"From that moment on, my life was an open book:
'Happy Days Are Here Again!' "

"That's not a book, Fonz, that's a song," Richie said.

"Somewhere, it must be in a song book," Fonzie
said, looking toward the sideshow area again. He suddenly drew back. "JoJo the Dog-Faced Boy?" he said.
"What kind of a nerd would let anybody call him a
dogface?—unless he was in the army."

"I guess he must be funny-looking," Ralph said.

"If that's all it takes, how come you don't have a
sideshow named after you?" Fonzie asked him.

"I'm not funny-looking!" Ralph protested.

"To who?"

Ralph thought for a second. "To my parents," he replied. "I'm not funny-looking to my parents."

"You got me there," Fonzie conceded. "If your
parents knew what you looked like, they would have
left home." His eyes returned to the canvas that
advertised JoJo The Dog-Faced Boy. "Being funny-
looking is okay," he said. "In fact, everybody I know,
except me, is a *little* funny-looking. But putting it up

on a sign and selling tickets to it—" He shook his head. "That is the king of the nerds."

"Maybe he can't do anything else," Richie said.

"There's got to be *something* else he could do."

"Chase cars?" Ralph said. "There couldn't be much money in that."

Richie changed the subject. "Fonz, do you think you could stay in the ring a whole round with the Muskogee Mauler?" he asked.

Fonzie looked at him levelly. "Cunningham, that is not the proper way to ask that question."

"Oh, yeah—I'm sorry," Richie said. "Fonz, do you think the Muskogee Mauler could stay in the ring with you a whole round?"

"Put that way, the answer is maybe yes and maybe no," Fonzie replied. "If he's like most of these carnival fighters, it won't do no good to knock him out of the ring. He'll have a rubber head from being punched in it so much, and he'll bounce right back in."

"Are you going to challenge him?" Potsie asked.

"If they make it worth my while, I might," Fonzie replied.

"Yeah, you'll need some extra money if you're going to date all those dancers," Ralph said.

"What for?" Fronze asked. "Those hoochie-coochie dancers must make a pretty good salary. They don't need no monetary help from me."

At dinner that evening at the Cunningham house, the conversation revolved around the carnival.

"When I was a little girl I just loved to go to the carnival," Richie's mother, Marion, said. "What I liked most was the cotton candy." She frowned thoughtfully. "But lately it just doesn't taste the same."

"It's like everything else these days, Marion," Richie's father, Howard, said. "They probably make it out of nylon."

"I'm going on *all* the rides!" Joanie said.

"Dear, I'm afraid that will cost too much," her mother told her.

"Mother, I've *got* to go on all the rides."

Marion looked at her perplexedly. "You've *got* to? Why?"

Joanie looked suddenly sheepish. "It's personal," she said.

"Joanie, personal or not," Howard said, "we can't afford for you to go on *all* the rides. Besides, you'd be sick."

She smiled blissfully.

Howard addressed Marion. "Maybe I wasn't listening to myself," he said. "Didn't I just tell our daughter that she couldn't go on all the rides because it would make her sick?"

"Yes, I think that's what you said, dear," Marion replied.

"Then why does she look so happy?"

"She's at that awkward age, Howard."

"Fonzie has a pass to all the rides and sideshows and everything," Richie said. "They gave it to him for fixing their hoochie-coo—I mean, they gave it to him for fixing their bus."

"Oh, my," Marion said distastefully, "is this one of those carnivals with the hoochie . . . that is, with the . . . uh . . . the . . . uh, the interpretive dancers?"

"Interpretive dancers, Marion?" Howard asked.

"Yes. The kind of dancers who tell a little story with their movements."

Howard nodded. "If my memory of hoochie-coochie dancers serves me correctly, you're on the right track," he said.

"Right track, wrong story," Fonzie said.

"Ahhh ... speaking of the carnival," Howard said, "I have a little news for you all. I was elected the entertainment and education chairman of the Boosters Club at our luncheon meeting today."

"That's wonderful, dear!" Marion said. "And you deserve it. You're one of the most entertaining men I know."

"Dad, what's that got to do with the carnival?" Richie asked.

"I'm getting to that," Howard replied, suddenly showing signs of nervousness. "You see, as chairman of the committee, the first speaker I signed up was Dr. Fenton Wilson."

"You work fast," Fonzie said. "You was only made the chairman at lunch, you just told us."

"Well, actually, it wasn't as fast as it sounds," Howard said. "Dr. Fenton Wilson is also a member of the Boosters Club. He was sitting right next to me at the meeting. I just turned to him and asked him."

"Dr. Fenton Wilson . . . he's the high school gym teacher, isn't he?" Marion said. "Why do they call him 'Doctor?'"

"He has a doctor's degree in physical education," Howard explained.

"Oh. That's nice. You mean he only treats boys and girls who hurt themselves in gym?"

"No, Marion, he isn't that kind of doctor, he doesn't treat anyone for anything. He just teaches gym—but on a very high educational level."

"Howard, I don't understand."

"Mom, when you're late for gym and you show up

without a pass, he never says 'Why *ain't* you got your pass?'" Richie said.

"Oh. Well, that makes sense," she responded, satisfied.

"Dad, you still haven't told us what the Booster Club has to do with the carnival," Joanie said.

"I'm getting to that." Howard got out his handkerchief and dabbed perspiration from his forehead.

"Are you too warm, Howard?" Marion asked. "I hope you don't have a fever."

"I'm fine," he said, putting the handkerchief away.

"What's this high school gym teacher that ain't no doctor gonna talk on?" Fonzie asked Howard, looking at him sideways. "Hoochie-coochie dancers?"

"No!" Howard replied quickly. "His subject will be 'The Romance of Anatomy.'"

"That sounds like hoochie-coochie dancers to me," Fonzie said.

"No, Fonz, anatomy is the structure of the body," Richie said. "You know, the bones, the muscles, all that."

"I know what anatomy is," Fonzie replied. "And I know what romance is. Put them together, anatomy and romance, and you got a hoochie-coochie dancer."

"As a matter of fact," Howard said, getting out the handkerchief again, "Dr. Wilson *will* be using some visual aids with his lecture."

"Howard ... what *kind* of visual aids?" Marion asked suspiciously.

"Marion, let me explain it to you the way Dr. Wilson explained it to me. You see, the human body is a very complex machine." He dabbed perspiration from his forehead again. "The foot bone, for instance, is connected to the ankle bone, and the ankle bone is connected to the thigh bone, and the thigh bone—"

"I *know* the song, Howard," Marion said. "What I *want* to know is what *kind* of visual aids."

"Human bodies, I suppose you might call them."

"*Whose* human bodies?"

"That is where we had a stroke of luck," Howard said. "It seems that Dr. Wilson has been noticing the carnival advertisements that have been posted up around town. In some of these advertisements there are some human bodies that are ... ahhh ... they are—"

"Doing the hoochie-coochie," Fonzie supplied.

"That *is* one way of putting it," Howard said. "As Dr. Wilson described it to me, though, these human bodies are performing experiments in stress and coordination, using their human bodies as a living laboratory."

"Yeah, that's the hoochie coochie," Fonzie said, nodding.

"Howard!" Marion said.

"Now, Marion, remember, I'm the educational chairman as much as I'm the entertainment chairman. This is going to be an educational lecture."

"He's right, Mrs. Cunningham," Fonzie said. "You can learn a lot from hoochie-coochie dancers."

"If I had anything else in mind, Marion, would I be taking you to the carnival with me tonight?" Howard said.

"We're going to the carnival? You didn't mention that."

"Well, I'm mentioning it now."

"*Why* are we going?"

"Because you like cotton candy," Howard replied.

"And also—just incidentally—because I have to make arrangements with the—the, uh—"

"Human bodies," Richie said.

"Yes, the human bodies ... that is, the young ladies. I have to make arrangements with them to appear at the Booster Club luncheon next week."

"Let someone else do it," Marion said icily.

"Dear, I can't do that. I'm the chairman. The chairman has certain responsibilities. You wouldn't want me to shirk my responsibilities, would you?"

"Yeah, Mom, what if Martha hadn't let George go to Valley Forge?" Richie said. "Today, we'd all have English accents. Nobody would be able to understand anybody."

"Dad *wants* you to go with him, Mom," Joanie pointed out. "So what could happen?"

"It isn't what could happen tonight that worries me," Marion replied, "it's what could happen between now and when that carnival leaves town. When I was your age," she told Joanie, "the man who lived next door ran away with a carnival dancer."

"But Dad wouldn't do anything like that," Joanie said.

"Of course not," Howard said. "I've got too much invested in the hardware store."

"Anyway, Mrs. Cunningham," Fonzie said, "the hoochie-coochie dancers are going to be pretty busy this week. I've got them all dated up."

Howard stared at him. "*All* of them?"

"All that was on the bus. Any of them that was in hiding someplace don't count. I don't go *looking* for dates," Fonzie said. "Any that don't come to me, it's no deal."

"Well ... all right ... I'll go to the carnival with

you," Marion said to Howard. "But I won't feel safe again until those dancers are out of town. I remember what that man who lived next door to us told *his* wife just before he ran off."

"What?"

"He told her he was making plans for a second honeymoon."

"Well, evidently he was," Howard said. "He just failed to mention that he was taking someone else along and leaving her at home."

There was a knock at the door.

"That's probably Potsie and Ralph," Richie said, rising. "We're going to the carnival together."

"I'll help you clear the table, Marion," Howard said, getting up.

She burst into tears. "That's how it starts—being nice!" she said, running from the room.

Howard sighed wearily and trailed after her. "You'll have to clear the table, Joanie," he said. "I've got to explain this whole thing to your mother again."

When he had gone, Joanie leaned across the table and whispered to Fonzie. "Let me use your pass," she said. "Just for one night. I've *got* to ride on all the rides. Let me use your pass, and I'll do anything you ask. I'll—I'll shine your shoes for you every day."

"I wear boots," Fonzie told her. "And I don't shine them."

"All right, I'll do that for you," Joanie said.

"What? Not shine my boots? How lucky can I get?"

"Fonzie, please," Joanie said. "I've *got* to ride on all those rides."

"Shortstuff, what's so important about that? And besides, like your father told you, you'd get sick as a dog."

"I *know!*"

"Huh?"

"Fonzie, have you noticed anything different about me lately?"

He looked at her closely. "Has your nose always been right there in the middle of your face?"

"Fonzie, be serious!"

"I'm serious. I thought it used to be over to the left a little."

"I'm on the verge," Joanie told him, whispering again.

"Today, I'm a girl, but tomorrow—or whenever—I'll be a woman."

"Yeah I think that's how it works," Fonzie replied, not particularly impressed.

"But for it to happen, something really nauseating has to happen first," Joanie said.

Fonzie studied her for a second. "Who told you that?" he asked.

"Somebody who *knows!*"

"Who?"

"My girlfriend."

"Oh . . . okay, as long as you got it from an expert."

"It happened to her," Joanie said. "She went to a church dinner where they served veal scallopini and that night, after, she was really sick. *Really* sick. But then, when she woke up in the morning, it had happened. She was a *woman!*"

"Heyyyyyyy. You don't need my pass," Fonzie said. "What you want is some veal scallopini."

"No, it wasn't that."

"No? What do you think? She did something in church that offended God and He blasted her?"

"It was being sick—*really* sick—that did it," Joanie

told him. "You know, you need that jolt—like an electric shock or something—to get you over the hump from girlhood to womanhood."

"And you think going to the carnival and going on all the rides and getting really sick will do it?"

Joanie nodded. "So, please? Please let me use your pass?"

Fonzie hesitated. "I don't know . . . If you go to that carnival a girl and come home a woman and your mother finds out I had something to do with it, she's liable to kick me out of the house."

"Why? It's going to happen sooner or later," Joanie argued.

"Yeah, but mothers seem to be holding their daughters back longer these days," Fonzie said. "That's the only explanation I can figure out for bobby sox and saddle shoes."

"Fonzie, please, please, please!" Joanie said.

"Okay," Fonzie replied, getting the pass from his pocket. "Not only can you use it," he said, handing it to her, "but you get my blessing along with it. I hope you get good and sick."

"Thank you, Fonz," Joanie said. "And if I can ever do the same for you, just ask."

"Right. You owe me one really nauseating time."

Richie returned, accompanied by Potsie and Ralph.

"Fonz, can we talk to you?" Potsie said. "We've got an idea."

"It's his idea, Fonz," Ralph said, indicating Potsie. "That is, unless you like it."

"In that case, it's your idea too, I guess," Fonzie said.

"Something like that."

"I'll tell you right now," Fonzie said, "any idea that

came out of you two, together or separate, I don't like."

"That's fair," Ralph said. He turned to Potsie. "I told you it was a dumb idea."

"Listen, Fonzie, it's for your own good," Potsie said.

"You don't want to lose your natural immunity, do you?"

"My what?"

"Your natural immunity. Everybody has it—a natural immunity to disease germs. That's how we stay healthy, most of the time. Because we have this natural immunity to disease grems. But if we get weak and rundown, we lose it. Then the germs gang up on us—and wham!"

Fonzie turned to Ralph. "How come it sounds like one of your ideas?" he asked.

"You haven't even heard the idea yet, Fonz," Ralph said.

"I've heard enough of it to know it sounds like it come out of a head that dropped dead about a week ago and nobody's buried it yet."

"All we want to do is keep you from getting run-down and weak and losing your natural immunity, which is bound to happen if you don't share those hoochie-coochie dancers with somebody else," Potsie said.

"Aha! A light bulb just went on over my skull!" Fonzie said. "You want me to share the hoochie-coochie dancers with you and Ralph—right?"

"For your own good!" Potsie said.

"Tell you what I *will* share." Fonzie said. "I'll share my experiences with you. Someday, when you grow up, I'll tell you what happened with me and the hoochie-coochie dancers."

"But, Fonz, what about your health?" Ralph said.
"Germs are everywhere!" He suddenly pointed.
"There went one!"

"The last germ that tangled with The Fonz, its
wham backfired on it," Fonzie said. "It's still in the
hospital. The doctors use it to scare the other germs.
They tell them if they don't get out of the patients,
they'll sic The Fonz on them. How do you think patients in hospitals get well? Scared germs."

Marion burst into the room, looking pale.

"Mom! What's the matter?" Richie asked.

"That man who lived next door and ran away with
the carnival dancer!" she said. "I can see him just as
plain as if it were yesterday! The morning he left, he
had a flower in his buttonhole!"

"So?" Richie said.

Howard appeared, smiling innocently. "Everybody
ready to go to the carnival?" he asked.

He was wearing a flower in his buttonhole.

TWO

Richie and his parents with Fonzie and Ralph and Potsie stood on the ground and watched Joanie reach the top of the Ferris wheel.

"She ought to get off," Marion said painfully.

"Not while she's up there," Howard said.

"Yeah, that first step is a killer," Fonzie threw in.

The seat that Joanie was occupying began its descent.

"Maybe she'll ask the attendant to stop it so she can get off," Marion said.

"I don't think so. She still looks like a girl to me," Fonzie said.

The others looked at him quizzically.

"Is there anybody here she don't look like a girl to?" Fonzie asked.

The others shook their heads.

"Then there's no argument," Fonzie said.

Joanie's seat was reaching the bottom of the turn. Joanie waved—feebly.

"She's all right," Howard said. "She doesn't look any greener than she did when she got off the last ride."

"Green could be her natural color, only we never noticed it before," Fonzie suggested.

The others peered at him again.

"Well, we've never seen her under carnival lights before," Fonzie pointed out.

Joanie was on her way up again.

"Howard, we really ought to ask her to get off," Marion said. "This is her fifth ride."

"Marion, for some reason that I don't understand, Joanie seems determined to get sick. If it's what she really wants, I don't see how I can deny it to her. Anyway, getting a little sick won't hurt her. What could happen?"

"If she gets *too* sick," Fonzie said, "she might go right past where she's headed and turn into a frog."

"Fonzie, do you know something that we don't know?" Howard asked.

"Do you know how to rebuild a transmission?" Fonzie asked.

Howard shook his head."

"Then I know something you don't know," Fonzie told him. He turned to Richie, Potsie and Ralph. "Are you guys gonna stand around here and wait for that wheel to stop and a frog jump off, or are we gonna take in the sights?"

"Yeah, Mom, Joanie is all right," Richie said to Marion. "She doesn't have to be watched."

"And I've got to talk to those young ladies and make that arrangement," Howard said. "Of course, if you want to stay here and watch Joanie, I suppose I could talk to the ladies alone."

"I'll go with you, Howard," Marion said. "Joanie doesn't look at all ill to me."

Howard and Marion set off through the crowd in

the direction of the Isles of Paradise. Fonzie looked
up toward the top of the Ferris wheel, sent up a
salute to Joanie—who waved weakly in reply—then
led Richie, Potsie and Ralph toward the sideshows.

"Ahhh ... smell that smell!" Fonzie said rhapsodi-
cally, taking in a deep breath.

"Yeah, that's great," Potsie said. "That's the smell
of romance, adventure!"

"What it is," Fonzie told him, "is the smell of stale
grease—burning."

They halted at the tent of JoJo The Dog-Faced
Boy.

"Let's go in," Ralph said.

"I don't want to see no guy making a nerd of himself," Fonzie said.

"I want to find out what kind of a dog he looks
like," Ralph insisted.

The ticketseller called out to them. "Hey-ya, hey-
ya, hey-ya! See JoJo The Dog-Faced Boy! Watch him
scratch his fleas!"

"You know what they call that guy," Potsie said,
indicating the ticketseller. "He's a barker. At this
sideshow, they've got a barker outside and a barker
inside."

"Your sister is wasting her time on those rides,"
Fonzie said to Richie. "She ought to come over here.
This is the most sickening place I ever been."

"Come on, Fonz, let's go in," Ralph said.

"I'll go in," Fonzie replied. "But only so I can tell
this nerd what I think of a nerd that runs down his
own face."

They bought tickets and entered the tent. JoJo was
seated on a chair on a small platform. He was a fairly

young man. His face had a certain bulldogish look to it. Around his neck was a dog collar. Standing in front of the platform was a trio of rough-looking men who were taunting JoJo with comments.

"Let's see you chase your tail," one of the men said.

The other two cackled with laughter.

JoJo smiled thinly.

"I was wrong," Fonzie said. "There's not just one nerd in here, there's four nerds."

"Let's see you scratch your fleas," one of the men said to JoJo. "That's what we paid for."

JoJo, looking somewhat grim, scratched himself under his arms.

The same man picked up a small stick from the ground and tossed it out through the tent opening. "Go chase it!" he commanded JoJo.

"I don't do that," JoJo replied tightly.

"Go chase it," the man said again. "You're a dog, aren't you? That's what a dog does. Go chase it."

"No," JoJo answered.

"I want you to go chase that stick," the man said threateningly. "I paid my money to see a dog. I want to see a dog chase a stick."

"That's nothing," Fonzie broke in. "Just like it's no news when a dog bites a man, it's no big deal when a dog chases a stick. What is a big deal is when a *man* chases a stick."

The man glared at Fonzie. "Who asked you, buster?"

Fonzie stepped up to him. He put a boot on the man's foot, anchoring him to the ground, then stepped closer, backing him up against the tent pole.

"I want to see you chase that stick," Fonzie told the man.

The man looked at his two friends, then he looked at Richie, Potsie and Ralph.

"I'll count for you," Fonzie told him. "There is three of you and there is four of us."

"Four of us and a big dog," Ralph told the man.

The man shrugged indifferently. "We were leaving anyway," he said to Fonzie.

Fonzie backed away, releasing the man's foot.

"And don't bother to bring the stick back," Fonzie said, as the man and his two friends left the tent.

"What was that all about!" JoJo said angrily to Fonzie.

"Heyyyy!" Fonzie replied, surprised. "You *want* guys throwing sticks and making you run after them? You *want* guys treating you like a dog?"

"That's what I'm here for," JoJo replied. "Didn't you see the sign outside? What did you expect? I'm the Dog-Faced Boy!"

"I'll tell you something about that, too," Fonzie said. "You're a fake. I've seen cats that looked more like dogs than you do. All you got that looks like a dog is a pug nose."

"That's a lie!" JoJo said, incensed. "I'm a freak!"

"The only thing freak about you is in your head," Fonzie told him. "If you took down that sign outside, the only way anybody would know you had a face like a dog would be by that collar around your neck."

"Get out!" JoJo raged.

The ticketseller came rushing in. "What's going on in here?"

"Get this idiot out of here!" JoJo shouted. "He says I don't look like a dog!"

"What're you trying to do, ruin his career?" the ticketseller demanded of Fonzie. "That's his bread and butter. His face is his fortune." He made shooing motions. "Out! Out! Get outta here!"

"Come on," Fonzie said, motioning to Richie, Potsie and Ralph. "This is nerdsville!"

"Fonz, what was that all about?" Richie asked when they got outside. "I've never seen you so upset about anything before."

"I don't like to see no guy make a nerd out of himself," Fonzie replied. "If a guy is born a nerd, that's something else. But when he puts up a sign, saying he's a nerd, and then sells tickets to it, that gets my dandruff up!"

"It's his life, Fonz," Richie said.

"Yeah, yeah, yeah," Fonzie replied, cooling off a bit.

"But, you know, you're right," Potsie said, as they walked on. "Take that collar off and he wouldn't look much like a dog."

"It's the power of suggestion," Richie said. "You see a sign saying you're going to see somebody who has a face like a dog, then you go in and see this guy with a pug nose who has dog collar around his neck. You *think* you're seeing somebody with a dog-face."

"We ought to demand our money back!" Ralph said indignantly.

"Demand our money back!" Fonzie said, mocking him. "Don't you guys get it? It's not the hustle that bugs me. It's that guy sitting in there and letting other guys come in and tell him to go chase a stick. No human ought to do that."

"He ought to have more pride, you mean," Richie said.

"Yeah, whatever."

They suddenly found a beautiful, dark-haired, dark-eyed young woman standing in their way.

"Hi," she said seductively to Fonzie. "Nice to see you again."

"Oh, yeah—you were on the bus," Fonzie said. "Your mother is the witch."

"The gypsy fortuneteller," the young woman said, correcting him. "I'm Lola."

"Lola LaZonga," Fonzie said, savoring it. "That's a great name. It sounds like something rolling downhill." He introduced Lola to Richie, Potsie and Ralph, then looked her up and down. "And that something that is rolling downhill is going around a lot of curves," he added.

Lola smiled seductively again. "Would you like to have your fortune told?" she asked.

"To tell you the truth, I don't believe a lot in that stuff," Fonzie replied. "I figure the most anybody is going to see looking in a crystal ball is their own face looking back at them. But, why not? Good news never hurt anybody. And if it's The Fonz's fortune, it's got to be spectacular." He motioned. "Lead on," he said to Lola.

A few moments later, they entered Madame LaZonga's tent. Like her daughter, the fortuneteller was dark-haired and dark-eyed. The resemblance ended there. Madame LaZonga was short and pudgy. She was wearing a long, colorful silk dress and her head was wrapped in a bright silk scarf that was tilted slightly to one side, as if she had put it on in a hurry. Her manner was somewhat confused.

"Oh, yes—you repaired our bus," she said to Richie when she was introduced to him.

"No, that was Fonzie," Richie replied.

Madame LaZonga turned to Potsie. "Of course! Now I remember you," she said.

"This is the witch that's going to tell my fortune?" Fonzie said. "She wouldn't know my fortune if it came out in the newspapers, printed on page one."

"Mother, *this* is Fonzie," Lola said, pointing to him.

Madame LaZonga squinted at him. "Well . . . if you insist," she replied to her daughter. She sat down at a small table that was covered with a velvet cloth. "If you'll join me," she said to Fonzie, "we'll get started."

He sat down across from her, looking skeptical.

Madame LaZonga peered down at the tablecloth. "The crystal ball is cloudy tonight," she said. "We must be going to have rain."

"Mother, you don't have the crystal ball," Lola said, picking it up from the top of a nearby trunk. "You were using it as a weight, flattening out those wadded-up dollar bills—remember?" She placed the crystal ball on the table.

"Well, I'm glad the weather's cleared up," Madame LaZonga said. She looked deep into the crystal ball. "I see you riding a motorcycle," she said to Fonzie. She suddenly covered her ears. "Those motorcycles are so noisy!"

"That's you, Fonz!" Ralph said. "You're on your bike."

"Yeah, she can really see things in that crystal ball!" Potsie said.

"She saw me on my bike when I stopped to fix the bus," Fonzie said. "That's how come she knows I ride a bike."

"I see romance in your future," Madame LaZonga said.

"She knows I'm dated up with the hoochie-coochie dancers," Fonzie said.

"No, this is *true* romance," Madame LaZonga said. "Wait a minute . . . I see the girl . . ."

Fonzie leaned forward, peering into the crystal ball. "I think that rain is back," he said.

"She's a beautiful girl!" Madame LaZonga told him.

"Naturally. It's The Fonz's fortune. If any kind of girl but a beautiful girl got in there, the crystal ball would break."

"Her name is . . . her name is . . . I can't quite make it out," Madame LaZonga said. "But I can see her first initial . . . it's . . . it's . . . it's 'L'."

"She wearing a costume with a big 'L' on it, like Superman with his big 'S'?" Fonzie asked

"She has dark eyes and dark hair," Madame La-Zonga went on. "And her mother likes sweets."

Lola picked up an open box of candy from the trunk. "Want one, Mother?"

Madame LaZonga chose a piece. "I love sweets," she said.

"Hey 'L'!" Ralph said. "Maybe the 'L' is for Lola!"

"Me?" Lola said, looking surprised.

"How come I got the feeling that my fortune was already told before I even stepped into the tent?" Fonzie said.

"This girl would make a *wonderful* wife," Madame LaZonga said.

"Take a closer look in that crystal ball," Fonzie said. "I don't think that's me you see in there. What kind of bike is the guy riding?"

"Two-wheeled," Madame LaZonga replied.

"That could be me," Fonzie conceded. "What else do you see?"

"You live in a house."

"Big house or little house?"

"Medium-size house," Madame LaZonga answered.

"Who lives in the house with me?" Fonzie asked.

"Just a minute . . . Yes . . . yes, it's becoming clear
. . . I see you in the house . . . you're not alone. I see
. . . I see . . . I see . . . People! People live in the house
with you!"

"That's you, Fonz!" Ralph said. "You know who
those people are, don't you? That's Richie and Mr.
and Mrs. Cunningham and Joanie."

"It's becoming more and more clear," Madame La-
Zonga said. "I'm beginning to see the names of the
people. There's . . . there's Richie . . . and a girl, her
name is . . . it's Joan! Wait! I see two other names . . .
A Mr . . . No, a Mr. and a Mrs. The names are . . . the
names are Mr. and Mrs. Bumpingham!"

"Cunningham," Ralph said.

"Oh, yes . . . Cunningham . . ."

"That's them!" Ralph said, elated. "She saw them!"

"Yeah, I saw them, too," Fonzie said dryly, getting
up. "They had the mailman in there with them in
that crystal ball. They were telling him they wouldn't
take no more mail addressed to nobody named
Bumpingham."

"Next!" Madame LaZonga said to Richie.

"I'm sort of like Fonzie," he said, "I don't really
believe—"

Lola gave him a nudge, bumping him into the
chair. Off balance, Richie sat down.

"I see a medium-size house," Madame LaZonga
said, looking into the crystal ball. "Do you recognize
it?"

Richie also looked into the crystal ball. "I don't see
anything but snowflakes floating around," he said.

"I see someone else living this house," Madame La-Zonga said. "His name is Fonzie. Is that familiar to you?"

"That's the same house that—" Richie began.

"Now, you believe!" Madame LaZonga said triumphantly. She bent closer to the crystal ball. "I see money!"

Richie shook his head. "That couldn't be me."

"I *don't* see money!" Madame LaZonga said.

"Yeah, now, *that's* me," Richie said.

"What I see," she went on, "is someone very rich. You, Richie, are going to meet this someone very rich . . . and very soon . . ."

"I don't know anybody with a lot of money," Richie told her.

"This very rich person is a stranger to you," Madame LaZonga said. "I see you going on a trip. You are on your way to this rich person's home."

"Who's with him?" Ralph asked eagerly. "Is anybody with him? Is it me?"

Madame LaZonga suddenly straightened up. She stared dead ahead, her eyes glazed over. Then, abruptly, she became absolutely stiff, as if she were in shock.

"Hey! She was trying too hard!" Fonzie said. "She blew her fuses!"

"No, no, it's all right," Lola said. "Mother has been contacted by a spirit. In addition to being a fortune-teller, she is also a medium."

"Is that why she sees medium-size houses?" Fonzie asked.

"I mean she's a middlewoman between this world and the other world," Lola explained. "This always happens when a spirit makes contact with her."

"It must be the spirit of a slab of concrete, the way she's stiff like that," Fonzie said.

"Chester ... Chester ... yes, I hear you Chester ..." Madame LaZonga intoned, still rigid.

"She's talking to the spirit," Lola whispered to the others. "His name is Chester."

"We once had a cat named Chester," Potsie said. "I wonder ..." He leaned closer to Madame LaZonga. "Here, Chester—here, Chester ... here, pussy, pussy, pussy ..."

"My mother communicates only with *human* spirits," Lola told him testily.

Reluctantly, Potsie backed away. "I was sure for a second there that I heard a meowwww."

Madame LaZonga spoke up. "Yes, Chester, I understand. For a person of your position, that must be very embarrassing."

"I bet they're not letting him wear his underwear under his sheet," Fonzie said. He leaned toward Madame LaZonga. "Hey, Ches! Whatta you need? A pair of drawers?"

"He can't hear you," Lola told Fonzie. "He can only communicate with Mother."

"I know who he is," Potsie said. "He's an old vaudeville performer. I swear he was doing a cat imitation."

"Sshh!" hissed Ralph.

"I'll do what I can to help you, Chester," Madame LaZonga said. "But, you must understand, I'm a stranger in this town."

Silence.

Then Madame LaZonga spoke again. "Yes, perhaps I can enlist the assistance of my new young friends."

"I think a hunk of bait was just tossed out," Fonzie said.

"We'll help you!" Ralph said to Madame LaZonga.

"And I think some poor fish just grabbed it," Fonzie added.

"Thank you, Chester—and I'm sure you have a reputation for honesty, too," Madame LaZonga said.

"I think she's putting words in her own mouth," Fonzie said.

As suddenly as Madame LaZonga had gone stiff, she relaxed. Smiling, she sighed contentedly. "Such a lovely experience—going 'beyond' . . ."

"Yeah, I thought you went a little too far, too," Fonzie said.

"Who is Chester, Mother?" Lola asked.

"Chester Addams," Madame LaZonga replied. "He says he used to live in this town."

"Sure!" Potsie said. "Chester Addams! Rich Chester Addams! He died about a year ago."

"What does he want, Mother?" Lola asked.

"He wants to speak with his wife," Madame LaZonga answered. "He didn't tell me why. Evidently it's something very personal."

"His sheet's dirty. He wants to send his laundry home," Fonzie guessed.

Madame LaZonga addressed Richie. "Are you acquainted with Chester's wife?" she asked.

"Me? Know rich Mrs. Addams?" He shook his head. "Not me. I know where her mansion is. Everybody in town knows where rich Mrs. Addams lives. But I've never met her. I don't even know anybody—even second or third or fourth-hand—who's ever met her. I don't think she leaves the mansion much."

"Well, it's your fate to meet her now," Madame LaZonga told him. "You can't ignore fate."

"My fate how?" Richie asked.

"Don't you remember your fortune? You're going to go on a trip and meet someone who is a stranger to you and who is very rich."

"I don't get it," Fonzie said. He pointed to Ralph. "He's the poor fish that took the bait," he said. He next pointed to Richie. "But he's the fish that gets hooked."

"Fonz, maybe I ought to do it," Richie said. "I don't believe in spirits any more than you do, but ... you know ... maybe we're wrong."

"*You* could be wrong," Fonzie replied. "But let's keep this in the realm of reality. The Fonz couldn't be wrong."

Richie addressed Madame LaZonga again. "Okay, I'll go see rich Mrs. Addams and tell her Chester wants to talk to her."

"Can I have the same fortune as Richie?" Ralph asked the fortuneteller. "I'd like to go along with him. I've never met a rich stranger before."

Madame LaZonga waved a hand at him as if it were a wand. "Wish granted," she said.

"Me, too?" Potsie asked.

"You can go along on your friend's wish," she told him. "It's big enough for both of you."

"A two-seater," Fonzie said.

"Tell Mrs. Addams that I'll be happy to go to her mansion to conduct the seance," Madame LaZonga said to Richie.

"The what?"

"To make contact with Mr. Addams," Madame La-Zonga said. "In fact, it will probably be easier there. I'm sure he knows where the mansion is. But he told me he had trouble finding my tent in the middle of this carnival. He found himself in the Isles of Paradise tent at first—quite by accident, I'm sure."

"I'll go see rich Mrs. Addams first thing in the morning," Richie promised.

Madame LaZonga touched a hand to her brow and sighed deeply. "These journeys to the 'beyond' exhaust me," she said.

"Let's let Mother recover," Lola said, motioning the others out of the tent.

When they were outside, Lola drew Fonzie aside to speak to him in private.

"What has Fonzie got that I haven't got?" Ralph asked enviously.

"A fortuneteller's daughter and more hoochie-coochie dancers than he'll ever be able to use," Potsie replied. He pointed into the crowd. "There's your father and mother and sister," he said to Richie. "At least, that's your mother. I'm not sure it's your father and sister."

The Cunninghams, sighting Richie, Potsie and Ralph, headed toward them. Richie's mother, looking fretful, was between his father and his sister, steering them. Howard's expression was dazed but happy. Joanie was green. Oddly, she appeared happy, too.

"You did it," Richie said to Joanie. "You went on one ride too many."

She nodded blissfully. "I'm sick. *Really* sick."

Fonzie joined them, having left Lola, who had gone back into the tent.

"I'm sick, Fonzie!" Joanie said. "Really sick!"

"Congratulations."

"Tomorrow," Joanie announced, "I'll be a woman!"

"Joanie, what is this nonsense!" Marion said. "I've

never seen anyone who was so sick who was so happy about it." She tugged at Howard's arm. "Howard, speak to her!"

·Howard smiled vacantly at his daughter. "Hi, Joanie," he said.

"Has he been on the rides, too?" Richie asked his mother.

"No! He's been to see the—the interpretive dancers," she replied.

Fonzie waved a hand in front of Howard's eyes. "You in there, Mr. Cunningham?" he asked,

Howard turned the vacant smile on Fonzie. "Richie, what are you doing behind the wheel?" he asked, still dazed. "I'm perfectly capable of driving this car."

"Yeah, he's looked at one hoochie-coochie dancer over his limit," Fonzie said.

"I've got to take him home," Marion said. "I've got to take them both home."

"Dad is in no condition to drive," Richie said. "I'll go along with you and make sure you get home safely."

"No, dear, I'm sure you have a lot more carnival to see," Marion said. "I'll take him home in a taxi. You and Fonzie can bring the car home later."

"Marion, I heard that," Howard said. "And you're absoluely wrong. I can drive. My mind is clear. My vision is clear," He began groping about perplexedly. "There's just one little problem," he said. "While we were at the carnival, someone stole the gearshift."

Marion blinked back tears. "I'm going right home and pack a bag," she said.

"Mom, you can't leave him just because he looked at one too many interpretive dancers," Richie protested. "Think about all the good years, when he didn't even look at *one* interpretive dancer."

"I'm not packing the bag for me," Marion replied. "It's for your father. I know what's going to happen tomorrow. He's going to run away with one of those dancers."

"Tomorrow," Fonzie told her, "he won't even want to ever see a hoochie-coochie dancer again. His eyes got so full they'll ache and they'll feel like the're as big as a barn."

"I hope so," Marion said. "But I remember that man who lived next door when I was a little girl. He *never* got his eyes full." She steered Howard and Joanie toward the exit. "Try to forget that you ever saw your father in this condition," she called back to Richie.

"Tomorrow!" Joanie shouted out as she was escorted away.

"What's going to happen tomorrow, I wonder," Richie said.

"A big change," Fonzie said.

"Yeah? What?"

"She'll only be about half as sick as she is tonight," Fonzie replied.

"Hey, Fonz, what did Lola LaZonga want to talk to you about in private?" Ralph said.

"Don't you know what the meaning of private is, nerd?"

"Sure. It means private. But you can tell me. I won't tell anybody."

Fonzie shrugged. "It's no secret," he said, walking on, joined by Ralph and Richie and Potsie. "She just said maybe I'd like to drop back around later, after the tent closes for the night."

"Wow!" Ralph said. "Drop back around for what?"

Fonzie glanced at him. "To play a little rummy with the fortuneteller cards," he replied. "What do you think drop back around for, nerd?"

"I guess you had to tell her you couldn't, huh, Fonz," Richie said.

"As a matter of fact, I didn't say yes and I didn't say no."

"But what about those hoochie-coochie dancers?" Potsie said. "You're dated up for tonight."

"Did you ever hear the story about the bird in the hand and the bird in the bush?" Fonzie asked him.

"The one about the bird in the hand being worth two in the bush?"

"That's a different story," Fonzie said. "The story I'm thinking about is where the guy has got one bird in his hand—which is like a fortuneteller's daughter—and then, later, he jumps in the bush and grabs off the other bird—which could be compared to a hoochie-coochie dancer."

"That's a lot of birds for one night, Fonz," Richie said.

"What's the point of being The Fonz if I can't perform spectacular feats?" He indicated Ralph. "I might as well be a nerd like him."

"Listen, I could handle a bird in the hand and a bird in the bush all in the same night," Ralph said. "I just don't get the opportunity, that's all. Give me a chance, Fonz. Let me keep your dates with Lola La-Zonga and those hoochie-coochie dancers for you!"

Fonzie shook his head. "The shock would be too much for the birds. They'd drop their feathers. I'll tell you what I'll do, though," he said. "I'll start you out on something your style."

"Great!" Ralph said. "Who?"

"It's not a who, it's a what," Fonzie replied. "You get the bush."

Ralph started to protest, then considered for a moment. "I'll take it," he said. "It's an improvement over nothing."

THREE

As Fonzie, Richie, Potsie and Ralph strolled idly along the carnival midway, their attention was drawn by loud cheering from the tent of the Muskogee Mauler.

"Maybe that was a knockdown!" Potsie said excitedly.

"It could have been anything from a knockout to a mile-wide miss," Fonzie said. "Guys at prize fights cheer anything. I saw guys at a prizefight cheer a ringpost once."

"Why would they do that?" Ralph asked.

"One of the fighters butted into the ringpost head-first and knocked himself out," Fonzie explained. "Since he was out, he couldn't be the winner even though he did it to himself. So the ring post got the decision."

Another rousing cheer came from the tent of the Muskogee Mauler.

"That sounds like a good fight," Ralph said. "Let's go in!"

"There is no such thing as a good carnival fight," Fonzie said, as they stopped in front of the tent. "The carnival fighter knows what he's doing and the local rubes that he's fighting don't. Anytime you see a good carnival fight, it's not because it's a good fight, it's because the carnival fighter is making it look good."

"Why would he do that?" Richie asked.

"To get the crowd to cheering and sucker in the suckers from outside," Fonzie explained.

Another loud cheer came from inside.

"That must be a *great* fight!" Ralph said.

"Suckers like him," Fonzie said to Richie, pointing to Ralph.

Richie looked up at the sign above the tent and read aloud:

WIN $10
STAY ONE ROUND WITH
THE MAULER!

"That is money!" Potsie said. "Ten dollars for three minutes' work! If you'd do that for a whole year, you'd be a millionaire."

"Do it, Fonz, do it!" Ralph urged. "*Ten dollars* for three minutes."

"What do you think the Muskogee Mauler is, some charity?" Fonzie responded. "You think he hands out sawbucks like it's paper money? He's not going to let no local rube stay a whole round with him. If some local rube gets lucky and stays even two minutes, the Mauler is then going to lower the load on him. The rube not only don't win the ten bucks, it costs him a pile to get his face moved back around to the front of his head."

"What did the Mauler do to it?" Ralph asked.

"He knocked it around to the back."

"You could do it, though, Fonz," Richie said. "You could stay in there for three minutes. Three minutes is nothing."

"If it's nothing, why don't you do it?" Fonzie asked him.

"I need my face where it is," Richie replied. "I don't want to see where I've been, I want to see where I'm going."

"Come on, Fonz, you can do it," Potsie said. "Ten dollars—that's a lot of money."

Fonzie considered for a second. "Well ... I'll give this Mauler a look-see," he said.

They bought tickets and entered the tent. Quite a number of men and one gray-haired woman were seated around the ring on bleachers. A fight was in progress, with the Muskogee Mauler, a bald mountain of a man, being challenged by a younger, smaller man, who was skipping about the ring as if he were dancing on hot coals. A small man in a checkered vest and a derby hat was acting as referee.

"If that guy can keep running he might stay the three minutes," Fonzie said, as he and Richie and Potsie and Ralph sat down near the gray-haired woman.

"Give him the old what-for, Sonny!" the woman bellowed.

Fonzie looked at her interestedly, then spoke to her. "Is that dancer in there your son?" he asked.

"Not the tippy-toe fella," she replied. "The Mauler—that's my son. I'm Mom Mauler." She pointed toward the ring. "The ref—that old dandy in the derby—that's Pop Mauler."

"I guess you could say the Muskogee Mauler is kind of a Mom and Pop operation," Fonzie commented.

"Durn tootin'!" Mom Mauler replied. She turned her attention back to the ring. "Go for his gut, Sonny!" she shouted.

In the ring, the dancer had danced himself into a corner.

"This is the end," Fonzie told Richie, Potsie and Ralph.

"He's fast—he could get out of there," Potsie said.

The dancer ducked to the left. The Mauler blocked the escape route with his body. The dancer tacked deftly to the right. But he found the Mauler in his way. The dancer ducked down. The Mauler swung overhand, as if he were wielding a sledgehammer, bringing his fist down on top of the dancer's head. The stunned dancer wobbled, then dropped.

The crowd roared.

"Kick him while he's down, Sonny!" Mom Mauler bellowed.

When the dancer had been dragged from the ring by his friends and the Muskogee Mauler had retired to his corner, Pop Mauler stepped up to the ropes and addressed the crowd.

"That was a lucky punch, folks!" he said in a raspy voice. "Three minutes is no time at all—only the hundredth part of an hour! Who is going to be the ten-dollar winner tonight? Step right up. In every town, there's always a winner! It could be *you!*"

"I'll take him!" a voice called out.

The crowd cheered.

A young man who was almost the size of the Mauler climbed into the ring, stripping off his shirt. He was provided with gloves, then the two fighters were motioned to the center of the ring by Pop Mauler and given instructions.

"What do you think, Fonz?" Potsie asked.

"This guy is big enough," Fonzie replied. "But is he smart enough? All that muscle is not much good if it don't have a brain to tell it what to do."

The bell rang and the fight began.

"Rip out his liver, Sonny!" Mom Mauler shouted.

The challenger swung wildly, missing. The force of the blow sent him spinning, out of control. He collided with the ropes and bounced off—and was met, chin high, by the Mauler's glove. The challenger stiffened, then dropped, out cold.

The crowd booed.

As the second young man was removed from the ring, Pop Mauler stepped up to the ropes again. "Another lucky punch, folks!" he said. "But luck can't last forever. The Mauler's time has come! Who'll be the the one to put him away? The time is ripe! He who hesitates is out ten bucks!"

"Go on, Fonz, try it!" Potsie urged.

"I'm thinking, I'm thinking."

"Go ahead, little fella," Mom Mauler said to Fonzie. "The Mauler won't hurt you. He's a teddy bear. I know—I'm his mommie."

"The Mauler is a teddy bear like a ten-ton tank is a tricycle," Fonzie replied.

"But you've got brains, Fonz," Richie said.

"Yeah, and I'd like to keep them where they are, not splattered all over that ring."

"It's big money, folks!" Pop Mauler called out from the ring. "Ten dollars for three minutes! That's more money than a college graduate makes! Step right up! Win your diploma in the manly art of self-defense!"

"That did it," Fonzie said, rising. "I'm a pushover for higher education."

The crowd cheered wildly as Fonzie was recognized.

"Ah! What have we here—a local celebrity?" Pop Mauler said, pleased.

"What you got is The Fonz," Fonzie told him, removing his jacket.

The cheer went up again.

"Are you a professional?" Pop Mauler asked, as Fonzie got out of his T-shirt.

"You could say that. I'm a professional Fonz."

The crowd whistled and stomped.

Fonzie climbed into the ring and was provided with a pair of gloves which Pop Mauler laced on for him. Pop and Fonzie and the Muskogee Mauler then moved to the center of the ring.

"No hitting below the belt," Pop Mauler told Fonzie. "Anything else goes."

"That's my kind of fight," Fonzie replied. "I don't like to be held back by no rules like no ripping out livers."

The two fighters went to their corners.

"Use your brains, Fonz!" Richie shouted.

"Use your elbows, Sonny!" Mom Mauler bawled.

The bell rang.

Fonzie and the Mauler moved to the center of the ring and began circling each other warily. The Mauler jabbed with a right, missing. The circling resumed.

"Trip him, Sonny!" Mom Mauler shouted. "He can't run when he's down!"

The Mauler lunged. Fonzie easily sidestepped the blow and the Mauler met with the ropes and bounced off—but came back lunging again. Once more, Fonzie evaded the charge. Then he and the Mauler squared off again.

"Fight! Fight! Fight!" the crowd began chanting.

Mom Mauler joined in. "Kill! Kill! Kill!"

The Mauler threw a hard left. Fonzie ducked under it and, moving behind the Mauler, went to the ropes and called down to Richie. "How many more minutes?"

"Two minutes to go!" Richie shouted back. "Fonz! Watch out!"

The Mauler was charging.

Fonzie raised a glove. "Hold it!" he said to the Mauler.

Surprised, the Mauler stopped.

"I would have ducked with you running at me like that," Fonzie told him. "You would have gone right past me and over the ropes. You could've hurt yourself." He squared off again. "Okay—now," he said. "But watch it with that running at a guy and going over the ropes. You're no pole vaulter, you're supposed to be a fighter."

The Mauler let go with a roundhouse right. Fonzie ducked. Then, as the Mauler's blow breezed by overhead, Fonzie pounded a left into his opponent's midsection. The Mauler stumbled backwards.

The crowd roared its approval.

"You monster!" Mom Mauler shrieked. "You struck my baby!"

Ignoring her, Fonzie called out to Richie again. "What's the time?"

"One more minute, Fonz!"

The Mauler, having recovered, attacked once more. He swung with a right, missing. He swung with a left, missing. He delivered the sledgehammer blow, missing, then followed it with a left uppercut, missing again. Fonzie, all the while, had hardly moved.

Half of the crowd booed and the other half cheered.

Fonzie stuck out his chin. "Right here—right on the button!" he said to the Mauler, offering his chin as an easy target.

Seemingly infuriated, the Mauler wound up and swung wildly—and missed.

The booing drowned out the cheering.

Raging and snorting, the Mauler aimed another roundhouse swing at Fonzie. Fonzie, stock still, studied it bemusedly as it breezed past his chin. The Mauler jabbed with a right, then a left, then a right, missing each time.

Fonzie strolled over to the ropes. "Tell him he shouldn't lose his temper," he advised Mom Mauler. "It throws his timing all off."

The bell rang.

Pop Mauler rushed across the ring and raised Fonzie's arm. "The winnah!" he announced, shouting to be heard over the wild cheering, stomping and whistling of the crowd.

"Fix!" Mom Mauler shrieked. "Fix! Fix! It was fixed!"

Pop Mauler began waving his arms, trying to quiet the spectators.

"Rematch!" Mom Mauler screamed. "Give us that palooka again! Rematch! We'll murder the bum! Rematch!"

The cheering, stomping and whistling began to abate.

"The luck was on the other foot this time" Pop Mauler shouted. "The local champion is the winnah!"

"Yeah, how about the ten bucks," Fonzie said.

"All right—you want a rematch, you'll get a rematch!" Pop Mauler announced.

"Heyyyy! They didn't say that!" Fonzie told him. "That was Mom Mauler, the shill, that said that."

"A ten-rounder!" Pop Mauler said. "The Fonz versus The Muskogee Mauler!"

The crowd began cheering again.

"Hold it!" Fonzie protested.

"With a prize of a hundred dollars to the winner!" Pop Mauler announced.

"Don't hold it!" Fonzie said.

"And I personally will handle all bets that the local citizens want to place on the hero of the hour—The Fonz!" Pop Mauler told the crowd.

People began reaching for their wallets.

"The fight of the century will be held on the final night of the carnival!" Pop Mauler said. "That will give all the local citizens plenty of time to get down their bets!"

Some of the crowd began climbing into the ring, reaching money to Pop Mauler, eager to place their bets. Pop Mauler took a ten from a man and handed it to Fonzie.

"What game was you in before you got into the fight game?" Fonzie asked him. "The shell game?"

"Take your money and run," Pop Mauler advised him. "Just don't forget to show up on the last night of the carnival for the fight of the century. You're a sure winner. You handled the Mauler like he was a creampuff."

"If I win, you're going to be out a hundred bucks," Fonzie said. "You are also going to be out all the bets you are taking on your boy. I never knew of no fight promoter before who did business like that."

"It promotes good will," Pop Mauler told him. "We carnival people love to be loved." He began grabbing for the money that the men were reaching out to him. "Shower me with that love!" he said ecstatically. "Oh, yes, that green love! Fives, tens, twenties!"

Fonzie left the ring and rejoined Richie, Potsie and Ralph. Mom Mauler was also there.

"You put the hex on my baby!" Mom Mauler charged.

"Somebody put the hex on him," Fonzie replied. "The way his aim was, he couldn't have hit me if he'd been driving a truck."

"He'll get you next time!" Mom Mauler said irately, stomping off. "You're a dead ducker!"

"That's 'dead duck'!" Ralph called after her.

"No, she's right, I was doing a lot of ducking in there," Fonzie said, putting on his T-shirt. "But, next time, I think I could be dead."

"What do you mean?" Richie said. "He couldn't even touch you, Fonz. You were too fast."

"He didn't have any trouble touching that first guy we saw him fight," Fonzie said, getting into his jacket.

"But that guy wasn't The Fonz," Ralph said.

"He didn't have any trouble touching that second guy, either," Fonzie said, leading the way out of the tent.

"That guy wasn't The Fonz either, Fonz."

"Anybody carrying a haddock in his pocket?" Fonzie asked, as they left the tent.

"Fonz, why would any of us be carrying a haddock?"

"All I know is," Fonzie replied, "I smell a fish."

"Are you talking about the fight?" Richie asked.

"If nobody is carrying around a haddock, it must be the fight I smell."

"But you won!" Potsie said.

Fonzie shook his head. "I didn't win."

"Sure you did. You got the ten dollars, didn't you?"

"I didn't win," Fonzie insisted. "What I did was, I didn't lose."

"Is there a difference?" Ralph asked.

"Yeah. When you win, you win because of something you do. When you don't lose, you don't lose on account of something the other guy *didn't* do," Fonzie explained.

"You must have said that too fast," Ralph said. "I didn't understand it."

"Here's the thing," Fonzie said, halting. "The Mauler could have nailed me. He used a very unfair tactic. He had me wondering why he was swinging at me and not hitting me. I was confused. But he *didn't* nail me. Why not?"

"You were too fast for him," Richie said again.

"I was standing still," Fonzie reminded him.

"The Mauler needs glasses," Potsie guessed.

"The reason he didn't hit me was because he didn't *want* to hit me," Fonzie told them. "The fight was a setup."

"If it was a setup, it backfired," Ralph said. "It cost them ten bucks."

"Use your brain, brainless," Fonzie said. "That ten bucks is going to come back to them like bread on the water—*heavy bread.*"

"How so, Fonz?" Richie asked.

"Think! What is going to happen next? There is going to be another fight. And there is going to be a lot of money bet on The Fonz—right? "

"Yes," Richie nodded.

"Do you know why the heavy betting is going to be on The Fonz? Because all those guys in there around that ring saw what happened in the first fight. They saw The Fonz breeze through it without even raising one drop of perspiration—and win. They figure the big fight will be the same, a sure thing for The Fonz. They figure their bets are safe. They figure they can't lose."

"*Can* you lose, Fonzie?" Potsie asked.

He nodded. "It could happen. I don't know how good that Mauler is. I didn't see him fight. He was carrying me. That was an act he was putting on, missing me with those roundhouse swings."

"Yeah, but you can beat him, Fonzie," Ralph said. "You're The Fonz."

"Yeah, and he's The Mauler," Fonzie said, walking on.

"But a Fonz is better than a Mauler," Ralph argued.

"You won't get no big international debate on that," Fonzie replied. "All I'm saying is that it's possible that he could get lucky and beat me. I remember what those gloves of his looked like when they were whizzing past me. If one of them had landed, I would have been sitting out there in the crowd on Mom Mauler's lap."

"Fonz, a lot of guys are betting a lot of money on you," Potsie said anxiously.

"Okay, okay, don't bug me. All I said was that it's *possible* that I could lose. *Anything* is possible. Shirley Temple grew up, didn't she? What were the odds on that happening? A trillion to one."

"Fonz, you've got to go into training," Richie said.

"For what? I'm already The Fonz. That's the peak. Guys that are in training are trying to reach some goal. How much higher can you go than the peak?"

"But you just said you *could* lose," Richie said.

"Sure, and Shirley Temple could shrink down to a midget again. But it won't happen."

"Fonz, this is serious," Richie insisted. "Those guys who are making bets on you don't know what's going on. They're depending on you—in good faith. You can't take a chance on letting them down. You've got to go into training."

"Doing what?"

"Running," Richie told him. "And lifting weights."

"Yeah, okay," Fonzie replied, as they left the carnival grounds. "If I come across any weights that look like they want lifting, I'll run." They had reached the Cunningham car. "You guys get in," he said. "I'll drive you home and pick up my bike. I got some heavy dates to keep. I'm not going to pick up no heavy date in a car. It wouldn't be The Fonz."

"Fonz, I hate to tell you this," Richie said, as they got into the car, "but no more dates. Not while you're in training."

Fonzie stared at him. "What am I supposed to be in training for, to be a monk?"

"Girls ruin your concentration," Potsie told him.

"You don't know how The Fonz operates," Fonzie replied, starting the car. "When I'm with somebody of the opposite sex, I concentrate."

"That's the point," Richie said. "You can't concentrate on girls and keep your mind on the fight."

"Cunningham," Fonzie said as they drove off, "I got to have a talk with you about what's important in life. Somehow, your education has been neglected. When it's a choice between a girl and a fight—leave it to the Marines."

"What?"

"Let somebody else do the fighting, you take the girl," Fonzie explained.

"Fonz, normally I couldn't agree with you more," Richie said. "But this isn't a normal situation. Everybody is depending on you. Everybody believes in you. They've bet their money on you."

"The money is safe. I can beat that Mauler. All I got to do is stay out of his way ... and then get lucky. One lucky punch, that's all it'll take."

"Boy, I'm glad I didn't have any money to bet," Ralph said.

"Heyyyy! What're you trying to do? Destroy my confidence?"

"You've got to go into training, Fonz," Richie insisted again.

"A little running couldn't hurt me, I guess," Fonzie said.

"We'll set up a program for you," Potsie told him. "Running in the morning, weight-lifting in the afternoon, and no dating at night."

"Something sounds a little wrong with that," Fonzie said.

"What?"

"I don't know. I can't put my finger on it. Tell you what," Fonzie said, "you guys do the program yourselves for a couple days—maybe a week or two—and if it works out for you, then I can try it. I don't want to jump into anything hasty."

"No, Fonz, you start tonight," Richie said.

"Start how?"

"With no dating," Richie told him. "When we get

home, you go right to bed. You need the sleep. That's
when the body manufactures energy and stores it
up—when you're sleeping."

"Not *my* body," Fonzie said. "My body is running
around in my dreams." They had reached the Cunningham house and he turned the car into the drive-
way. "Sometimes my body gets so tired running
around in my dreams at night, I can't get up in the
morning. You want that to happen?" He asked, stop-
ping the car and switching off the motor.

"We'll take the chance," Richie replied, as they got
out of the car. "Everything I've ever read about training says you need a lot of sleep."

"The guys that wrote that didn't have a hoochie-
coochie dancer waiting for them on one hand and a
fortuneteller's daughter on the other," Fonzie said.

"And food," Ralph said, as they walked toward the
house. "You've got to eat a lot of big meals, Fonz. A
lot of steaks. You better have a steak right now, before you go to bed."

"I'll make you a trade," Fonzie said. "I'll eat the
steaks and you do the running and the weight-lifting."

"Let's go to the kitchen," Richie said, as they entered the house. "Maybe I can find a steak."

"I'll go along with the steak idea," Fonzie said. "I
might be needing some extra strength tonight. If I
don't need extra strength, I will be *very* disappointed
in the sisterhood of hoochie-coochie dancers."

"Did you decide?" Ralph asked. "Is it going to be
the hoochie-coochie dancer instead of Lola LaZonga?"

"When I said hoochie-coochie dancer, that was a
figure of speech," Fonzie replied. "I could have meant
a hoochie-coochie dancer or a fortunetellers' daughter

or somebody else. When the Fonz talks about girls, he is speaking broadly."

Ralph nodded, signifying understanding.

"Laugh," Fonzie told him. "I just told a pun."

Ralph laughed. "I don't get it," he said.

Richie called over from the refrigerator. "No steaks. But there's plenty of milk. How about a bowl of cereal, Fonz?"

"I'll have a bowl of cereal," Potsie said. "What have you got?"

"Rice Krispies," Richie reported, looking into the cupboard.

"Nix!" Fonzie said. "The family is asleep. You want to wake them up with all that snap, crackle and pop?"

"Fonzie is right," Richie said. "If we can't find a steak for him, we better put him to bed."

"*Put?*" Fonzie said. "*Put* The Fonz to bed? Like some little kid in his Dr. Dentons and his flap hanging down? You're gonna *put* The Fonz to bed?"

"What I meant was, walk up to your room with you and make sure you go to bed instead of going back to the carnival," Richie replied.

"Okay. But don't never say you're gonna *put* The Fonz to bed. When The Fonz goes to bed, he puts himself." He led the way from the kitchen. "And if anybody's got any ideas about tucking anybody in, he can go stick his head in a bucket."

"What would be a good time for him to start his roadwork in the morning?" Potsie said to Richie, as they followed Fonzie down the hall.

"The earlier the better," Richie replied. "About six o'clock, I guess."

"There is no such time as six o'clock in the morning," Fonzie said.

"Sure there is, Fonz."

"How come I've never seen it?" he asked, heading up the stairs.

"I guess you've never been up early enough."

"For me and six o'clock in the morning, that's the perfect arrangement. I'm not going to be the one to spoil it."

"All right. Because tomorrow is the first morning, you can sleep in," Richie said. "We won't start roadwork until six-thirty or seven."

"Who's going to run with him?" Ralph asked, as they reached the upstairs hallway and walked toward Fonzie's room.

"We'll take turns," Richie replied. "I'll go first."

"Yeah, you go ahead," Fonzie said. "When it comes six-thirty or seven in the morning, you start running. When I get up, I'll catch up with you."

They entered Fonzie's room.

"Okay, turn in," Richie said to Fonzie.

"With you guys standing around watching me? Hasn't anybody ever heard of personal hygiene?"

As one, Richie, Potsie and Ralph nodded.

"We'll look the other way," Ralph said.

Fonzie roared at them. "Get out!"

They fled, bunching up on the doorway, then squeezing through and hurrying down the hall. Behind them, the door to Fonzie's room slammed.

"Boy, he's sure touchy about his hygiene," Potsie said.

Further along the hall, another door opened. Joanie peeked out, bleary-eyed. "Where are the elephants?" she asked.

"What elephants?" Richie asked puzzledly.

"I heard a whole herd of elephants going down the hall," she said, blinking into the light.

"That was us," Richie told her. "We were walking Fonzie to his room."

"I heard elephants."

"You're still sick," Richie said. "When you get better, we'll sound like us again."

Joanie nodded. "That's right, I forgot—I'm sick. I'm *really* sick," she said, smiling happily and closing the door.

"Your sister can be strange sometimes," Ralph said to Richie, as they walked on.

"She does that so we'll know she's a girl," Richie replied.

"Yeah, until they fill out, that's the only proof they have," Potsie said.

"Where are we going to get some weights for Fonzie?" Ralph asked, as they headed down the stairs.

"At the gym," Richie said. "We'll take him to the—"

From outside came the sudden roar of a motorcycle engine.

Richie, Potsie and Ralph halted.

"That couldn't be him," Potsie said. "How could he get outside? He didn't go past us."

"The window!" Richie said.

They raced back up the stairs and up the hall to the door of Fonzie's room.

"Fonz!" Richie called out, pounding on the door.

There was no answer.

"We've got to go in there," Ralph said.

"If we break into his room, he'll kill us!" Potsie said.

"We've got to go in!" Richie insisted. "We've got to find out if he's gone!"

Ralph shouted through the door. "Personal hygiene or not, here we come!"

Richie threw open the door and they charged into the room. The window was open. Fonzie was nowhere in sight.

"Not that I blame him," Ralph said. "When you've personal-hygiened yourself, it's a shame to waste it going to bed. Especially if you've got a hoochie-coochie dancer and a fortuneteller's daughter waiting."

They left the room and walked back down the hallway again.

Joanie's door opened a crack and she peeked out.

"Don't tell me *that* wasn't elephants!" she said. "I heard their motorcycles!"

FOUR

The Cunninghams were at breakfast when Potsie and Ralph arrived at the house the next morning. Howard was eating with his eyes closed. Joanie was not eating at all, she was staring glassily into space. Between bites, Marion kept glancing worriedly at her husband. Only Richie appeared untroubled.

Entering behind Potsie, Ralph closed the back door noisily.

Howard groaned and shuddered.

"Did I do something?" Ralph asked.

"His eyes have a hangover," Richie explained.

Potsie looked closely at Joanie. "What's the matter with her?"

"She hasn't told us yet," Richie replied. "But I think she's listening for those elephants to come back on their motorcycles."

"Hi, Mrs. Cunningham," Ralph said.

"Don't worry about me," Marion responded. "I'll take the children and go home to my mother."

"Marion," Howard said painfully, keeping his eyes closed, "I am not going to run away with any carnival dancer."

"Can you look me straight in the eyes and say that?"

"Marion, don't ask me to do that," Howard pleaded. "My eyes came unglued last night. If I open my eyelids, my eyes will fall out."

"Richie, did Fonzie do his running this morning?" Potsie asked.

Richie shook his head. "He's still in bed."

"Didn't you wake him at six-thirty or seven?" Ralph asked.

"I woke him. He's going to do the running later."

"Is that what he said?" Potsie asked.

"What he said, actually, was that if I didn't get out of his room and let him sleep he was going to throw me out of the room and up the hall and down the stairs."

"Yeah, that's Fonz—he meant he was going to do the running later," Potsie said.

"Are we going out to see rich Mrs. Addams?" Ralph asked.

"Rich Mrs. Addams?" Marion said. "What for?"

Richie told his mother about his fortune and about the visitation of Chester Addams' spirit to Madame LaZonga's tent. "So, because I don't want to make a liar out of my fortune," he said, "I'm going out to the Addams place to tell rich Mrs. Addams that Madame LaZonga is willing to hold a seance for her so she can talk to her husband."

"A seance!" Marion said excitedly. "I've never been to a seance!"

"I'll ask rich Mrs. Addams if you can sit in, Mom," Richie said.

"That would be lovely. I'd like to ask Mr. Addams

a question about angels. With those wings, I wonder if they're able to sleep on their backs."

"Marion, I don't think angels sleep," Howard said. "Besides, how do you know where old Addams is? There might not be any angels around. As I remember him, he was a crook."

"Mr. Addams! Why, he was the most respected man in town. Everywhere I go, I see a plaque, honoring him."

"He put those up himself," Howard told her. "Did you ever read the plaque on that big oak tree in the park? It says, 'Created by God in association with Chester Addams.'"

"The tree, did he mean?"

"I'm not sure," Howard replied. "He may have meant the world, but he couldn't figure out how to nail that plaque to the ground."

"Dad," Richie said, "is it okay if I drive you to work this morning, then use the car to go out to rich Mrs. Addams' place?"

"I insist on it," Howard replied. "My present schedule calls for me to keep my eyes closed until well into the afternoon."

"Well, at least that means you won't be running away from home with that carnival dancer before evening," Marion said. "I suppose we ought to be thankful for small favors."

Joanie moaned.

They all looked at her hopefully—all except Howard, who continued to keep his eyes closed.

"What is it, dear?" Marion asked Joanie.

"I think it's happening," Joanie replied.

"*What* is happening?" Marion asked testily. "You still haven't told us what you expect to happen."

"I'm becoming a woman!"

Marion looked shocked. "Not in front of your brother and his friends!" she protested.

Joanie hiccupped.

"False alarm!" Marion said happily. "It was only an air bubble."

Shortly after, Howard and Richie and Potsie and Ralph left the house and drove to the hardware store, then Richie and Potsie and Ralph drove on to the Addams mansion. It was surrounded by a high stone wall. They parked at the iron gate, which they found locked. Richie pressed the bell button. A few minutes later, a butler, a tall, middle-aged, distinguished-looking man, emerged from the mansion and approached the gate.

"Mrs. Addams does not wish to subscribe to any magazines," the butler told them.

"No, that's not why we're here," Richie replied. He then related the story of having his fortune told and of the later visitation to Madame LaZonga's tent of the spirit of Chester Addams.

"Horsefeathers," the butler said.

"Honest," Richie insisted.

"I served Mr. Addams for quite a number of years," the butler told them, "long enough to know that if his spirit went to a carnival, it wouldn't waste its time in the fortune teller's tent. It would head straight for the hoochie-coochie dancers."

"He went there first," Potsie said. "Later, he showed up at Madame LaZonga's."

"Bushwa!" the butler said. "Tell me what magazines you're selling so I can inform you once more that Mrs. Addams is not interested in subscribing to any magazines."

"We're telling the truth," Richie insisted again. "Mr. Addams is trying to get in contact with Mrs. Addams and he's using Madame LaZonga as the go-between."

"Well, whatever the magazines are, Mrs. Addams is not interested," the butler said, and he turned and strode off, disappearing into the mansion.

"Well, we tried," Potsie said.

"Why don't we call her on the phone?" Ralph suggested.

"We'd just get the butler," Richie said. He stepped back and looked up toward the top of the wall. "Boost me up," he said.

"That's trespassing!" Potsie said. "You could be arrested."

"I don't know this neighborhood," Richie replied. "I'll say I was lost and wandered over the wall by mistake."

"A six-foot wall?"

"He can say he was lost for hours and became delirious and thought the wall was a mirage," Ralph said.

Potsie shrugged. "I guess as long as you have a good story nothing can happen," he said to Richie.

Potsie boosted Richie up. When Richie was on top of the wall he reached down and pulled Potsie up, then they both reached down and pulled Ralph up. From the top of the wall they saw an enormous garden, with many different flowers in bloom. A plump, middle-aged woman in overalls and a large straw hat was working in the tulips.

"She must be the gardener," Potsie said. "But maybe she can tell us where we can find rich Mrs. Addams."

They jumped down from the wall and crossed the garden.

"We're looking for rich Mrs. Addams," Richie said to the woman in overalls. "Can you help us?"

Startled, the woman peered at them flusteredly. "What would you like me to do?" she asked.

"Tell us where we can find her."

The woman looked around, as if trying to establish her whereabouts. "I believe she's in the tulips," she told Richie.

"No, you're in the tulips," he said. "Who we want is—" A sudden realization struck him. "Are you rich Mrs. Addams?"

"I believe I am," she replied. "I was when I came out here. And I've always managed to get in and out of the tulips before without becoming someone else. Tulips, as a general rule, tend to their own business." She looked off into space. "Snapdragons, now, are another story," she said recalling. "Never bend over in a bed of snapdragons."

"We just didn't expect to find you in overalls," Richie explained.

"Protection against the snapdragons," she told him. She looked at him closely. "Do I know you, young man?"

Richie explained why he and Potsie and Ralph were there, telling her about his fortune and her late husband's desire to make contact with her through Madame LaZonga.

"Dear Chester," Mrs. Addams said, smiling fondly. Then she frowned. "Are you *sure* it was Chester? Did he offer any proof?"

"What kind of proof?"

"Did you hear change rattling?" Mrs. Addams

asked. "He always carried a pocket full of pennies to give away."

"Hey, I bet the kids liked him," Potsie said.

"He didn't give them to children. He gave them to waiters in restaurants as tips."

"I didn't hear any rattling," Richie said. "But, then, I don't think a spirit would have a pocket full of pennies. You know what they say: you can't take it with you."

"Oh, yes ... that's right ... That's why Chester fought so hard against dying."

"When he showed up in Madame LaZonga's tent, he said he'd just come from the Isles of Paradise," Potsie said. "Is that any—"

"It was Chester!" Mrs. Addams said, delighted. "How wonderful! Yes, tell Madame LaZonga I'll be very happy to have her conduct a seance here! Oh—and tell her to be sure and bring Chester."

"We'll tell her," Richie said. He and Potsie and Ralph headed off across the garden toward the gate.

"And I'll take the *Saturday Evening Post* and *The National Geographic*," Mrs. Addams called after them. "But don't tell my butler!"

FIVE

At noon, Richie, Potsie and Ralph arrived at the garage to start Fonzie on a training program for the fight. They were carrying a lunch for him. At first, they could not find him. Then Richie spotted his boots sticking out from under a car.

"Hey, Fonz!" he called.

There was no response.

Richie bent over and looked under the car. "He's asleep," he reported. He shook one of Fonzie's legs. "Fonz! Hey Fonz!"

For a second, there was still no reaction. Then Fonzie replied, fuzzily, "Cunningham, get out of my room, or I'll kick you out the door and up the hall and down the stairs."

"Fonz, you're not in your room. You're at the garage, under a car."

"Oh . . . yeah . . ." Slowly, Fonzie emerged. He blinked at the light. "I was catching eighty winks," he said.

"That's forty winks, Fonz."

"Forty winks that I lost last night and forty winks that I'm going to lose tonight," Fonzie said.

"Which one did you date, Fonz?" Ralph asked. "The hoochie-coochie dancer or the fortuneteller's daughter?"

"Both."

"Both? How could you do that?"

"I had my bike with me, didn't I? I rode it back and forth between them."

"We brought you a training lunch," Richie said, removing the lid from the small wicker basket he was carrying. "And after you eat, we'll do some running."

Fonzie looked into the basket. "Carrots?" he said. "Lettuce? Celery? What am I supposed to be, a rabbit?"

"We were going to bring you a steak," Potsie said, "but we couldn't figure out how to keep it hot. We didn't think you'd want to eat a cold steak."

"Celery?" Fonzie said again, appalled.

"Mom says all this stuff is good for you," Richie told him.

"Then let your mother fight the Mauler. I go to Arnold's for my lunch. Arnold knows what food is. Food is a hamburger and mustard and catsup. Celery is not food. Celery is thick grass!"

"Maybe you're just not hungry yet," Ralph said. "Why don't you do your running first? If you run far enough and long enough, you'll be hungry enough to eat anything."

"Running is for morning," Fonzie said. "It's too late now."

"Running is for anytime," Richie said. "Fonzie, you've got to get in shape. Big money is being bet on you. The word is out, everybody in town knows about the fight. And they're all betting on you.

Fonzie sighed wearily. "Okay, okay, I'll run, I'll run."

"You can run around the garage," Richie said.

"Once? Twice?"

"A hundred times at the least," Richie said. "It won't do you any good until you reach the point where you feel you can't run another step—but you keep going."

"Somehow, that doesn't sound like me," Fonzie said, leading the way out of the garage. "Most of the time I got brains enough to know when to quit."

Outside, Fonzie closed his eyes against the glare of the bright sunlight. After a second, he seemed to slump.

"Fonz . . ." Richie said.

Silence.

"He's asleep again," Potsie said. "He shouldn't have closed his eyes."

Richie shook him. "Fonz!"

"Yeah! Yeah!" Fonzie said, startled, awakening. "How many times around the garage is that?"

"You haven't even started yet."

"How come I'm so tired? I must have been running in my sleep."

"Have a carrot," Ralph suggested. "It'll give you strength."

"I'm not *that* tired," Fonzie said, setting out, jogging. "I'll *never* be that tired."

He disappeared around the corner of the garage.

"We'll take turns counting the laps," Richie said, as he and Potsie and Ralph sat down in the garage doorway. "A hundred laps—that's thirty-three-and-a-third laps apiece." He held out the wicker basket to Ralph. "Have some celery."

Ralph helped himself to a stalk. "I may need it," he said. "I've never counted to thirty-three-and-a-third before in one sitting."

Potsie took a carrot from the basket. "These are good for the eyes," he said.

Richie looked at him skeptically. "How do you know that?"

"Did you ever see a rabbit wearing glasses?"

Fonzie appeared from around the far corner of the garage, still jogging.

"One," Richie said, as he approached.

"Yeah, I must be one," Fonzie said. "A guy would have to be one to do this."

"I was starting the counting," Richie told him. "Ninety-nine to go."

"All the way around ought to be two," Fonzie complained. "Once around the back and once around the front. One and one is two."

"Fonz, this is for your own good," Richie said as Fonzie passed by. "You know how bad you'd feel if you lost to the Mauler because you weren't in shape."

"How do you think I'm going to feel when I'm too tired from running to even show up for the fight?" Fonzie answered. "Even worse, how do you think I'm going to feel tonight when I'm too tired to show up—"

He disappeared around the corner.

"I didn't hear that," Ralph said, taking another stalk of celery. "What did he say?"

"I didn't get it either," Potsie said.

"Something about tonight," Richie said.

Fonzie reappeared from around the far corner. "—for hoochie-coochie number two and the fortuneteller's daughter again," he said.

"Forget it, Fonz," Richie said. "Tonight, you rest— even if I have to stay up all night and stand guard under your window."

"Two," Ralph said.

"I'm doing the counting," Richie said, as Fonzie passed by once more. "You owe me a number. I get to count to thirty-four and-a-third."

"Oh, no!" Ralph objected. "The only reason I counted number two was because you weren't doing your job."

"You didn't give me a chance!"

Fonzie disappeared around the corner.

"You had *plenty* of chance!" Ralph told Richie. "You're not getting one of *my* numbers."

"Okay, Potsie," Richie said, "who's right, him or me?"

"Why don't you split number thirty-four," Potsie suggested. "Richie, you can say 'thirty', and Ralph, you can say 'four'."

"That's okay with me," Richie said.

"I don't know . . ." Ralph said.

Fonzie reappeared, making another circuit.

"Oh, hey, Fonz, we talked to rich Mrs. Addams this morning," Richie said. "She says it's okay for Madame LaZonga to hold the seance at the mansion."

"I'll tell her when I see her," Fonzie replied, passing by.

Richie turned to Ralph. "How about that deal, splitting number thirty-four?"

Fonzie turned the corner again.

"I'm still thinking," Ralph replied to Richie. "By the time we get to twenty-five, I'll have a decision.

From behind the garage came the roar of a motorcycle engine.

"He's headed for Arnold's!" Richie said, leaping up. "Let's go!"

Arriving at the carnival grounds, Fonzie parked his motorcycle at the entrance, then walked toward the fortuneteller's tent. On the way, however, he came upon JoJo the Dog-Faced Boy sitting outside his tent, whittling.

"Heyyyy!" Fonzie said. He pointed to the carving in JoJo's hand. "That's good! What is that? That's the Muskogee Mauler, isn't it? It looks just like him!"

"Go away!" JoJo said crossly.

Fonzie looked at the carvings that were lying on the ground beside JoJo. "That's the fat lady," he said. "And that's that guy that walks around on stilts, the tallest man on earth. What's that, an elephant? I haven't seen any sideshow around here with an elephant in it—not counting the fat lady."

"I was with a circus once," JoJo said.

"That's good knife work," Fonzie told him. "You could sell that stuff. You know what you could be?" he said. "You could be a guy that sits around and cuts up stuff out of sticks."

"A sculptor?"

"Whatever."

JoJo shrugged indifferently.

"Guys get famous doing that," Fonzie told him. "One guy got so famous doing it, they painted a picture of his old lady and hung it in a museum."

JoJo looked at him dubiously.

"I saw a picture of the picture," Fonzie said. "It's called 'Whittler's Mother.'"

JoJo laughed.

"Look at you," Fonzie said. "When you let your face crack up a little, you look like anybody else. The reason they call you Dog-Face is because you never smile. Did you ever see a dog smile? They want to, but they haven't got anything to smile about. Who would, leading a dog's life?"

JoJo laughed again. Then, looking down at the carvings, he scowled once more. "They're not good enough," he said.

"What you need is some Fonz," Fonzie informed him.

"What's that?"

"It's a state of mind," Fonzie explained. "When you've got Fonz, you figure there isn't anything you can't do, and do it better than anybody else. And the gorgeous part is, you're right."

JoJo shook his head. "I can't think like that," he said. "I know it isn't true."

"There's your problem—the thinking," Fonzie said. "If you think, your Fonz self-destructs. You have to do, not think. Save the thinking for later. Then, if you find out you couldn't do what you wanted to do, it's too late, you've already done it." He picked up a carving, studying it. "What you ought to do," he said, "is pack up and get out of here. Do you like this carving stuff? Then go someplace and get yourself a bunch of sticks and carve."

JoJo smiled again, softly this time. "I'd like that," he said.

"It's never too early," Fonzie said. "Don't even pack your bag, just get up and go."

"How would I live?" JoJo said nervously.

"Sell this stuff."

"What if no one wanted to buy it?"

"What if? What if? What if?" Fonzie replied crankily. "What if nobody had ever opened a gas station? I'd have to pull my bike with a horse. If you sit around worrying about 'what if', you'll never get anything done."

"But I don't have any problems here," JoJo argued. "I get paid every week and I have a place to sleep and a tent over my head when it rains."

"And a collar around your neck."

JoJo nodded. "I don't like that much."

"And guys coming in and throwing a stick out the door and telling you to go fetch it."

"There are a lot of people like that," JoJo admitted. He sighed wistfully. "Well ... maybe someday I'll leave ... but not today ..."

Fonzie put the carving down. "Those somedays are like fire extinguishers," he said, walking on.

"Like what?" JoJo called after him.

"By the time you find a fire extinguisher, the house is already burned down," Fonzie answered.

At the opening to the fortuneteller's tent, Fonzie halted and looked in. Madame LaZonga was there alone, seated at the small table, peering into her crystal ball and munching on chocolates.

"You are about to meet a handsome young man who has interesting news for you," Madame LaZonga said.

"Heyyyyy! What're you doing, telling your own fortune?" Fonzie called in.

"Oh—it's you!" she replied, peering out at him. "Yes, I keep in practice that way. What's the interesting news?" she asked, as Fonzie entered the tent.

"I haven't had lunch," he told her, taking a chocolate from the box.

"That *is* fascinating," Madam LaZonga said. "I'd rank it somewhere between the signing of the Magna Carta and the sinking of the Lusitania."

"Wherever," Fonzie replied, taking another chocolate.

"For how many days haven't you had lunch?" Madam LaZonga asked.

"Just today. I didn't have lunch today because I didn't want to meet some guys where I usually eat." He took still another chocolate. "They were chasing me with carrots and celery." He picked up another chocolate from the box. "Which reminds me," he said, "Rich Mrs. Addams wants you and Chester to come over to the mansion."

"Wonderful!" Madam LaZonga cried. "Wonderful for Chester, that is. He seemed to be very concerned about something. I'm sure it's important. Spirits don't came back from the beyond unless it's an emergency ... or a hoochie-coochie show."

Fonzie looked around. "Where's Lola?" he asked.

"She went into town to get me some more candy," Madame LaZonga replied. "Luckily," she added, as Fonzie took another chocolate. "Speaking of sweets," he said, "there's no sweeter girl in the world than my Lola. She— Oh, my!" she said suddenly, looking into her crystal ball.

"What happened?" Fonzie asked.

"I just saw you ride by," Madame Lazonga said.

"In that glass ball?"

"Yes. And Lola was riding behind you. I wonder what that means?"

"That's a rerun you're seeing," Fonzie told her. "It happened last night. I was down at the Isles of Paradise, seeing a hoochie-coochie dancer, then I came down here to see Lola, and I liked it better here, so I rode down to the Isles of Paradise on my bike to tell the hoochie-coochie dancer I wasn't coming back, and Lola went along behind, so that's what you're seeing in the glass ball."

"Seeing?" Madame LaZonga said dazedly. "I didn't even understand it."

"Look in the ball again. You'll see me and Lola coming back. But, after that, it gets personal."

Madam LaZonga peered into the crystal ball again. "There you go, you and Lola," she said. "But it isn't last night. I don't look back, I see into the future."

"It must be tonight," Fonzie said.

"No, you're much more mature," Madam LaZonga said. "And so is Lola. She looks happily married."

"Then that couldn't be me on that bike with her," Fonzie said. "I got a rule, I don't date other guys' wives."

"No, it's you," Madame LaZonga insisted, looking deeply into the crystal ball. "And there is something printed on the back of your jacket. It says—it says—I'm having a little trouble making it out ..."

"It says 'Get yourself a new crystal ball, this one has gone blooey,'" Fonzie said.

"No, it says—I can see it clearly now. It says 'Fearless Fonzie'."

"It sounds like me," Fonzie conceded. "But I still say it's not me."

"I see an advertisement!" Madame LaZonga said. "The carnival has a new star! It's Fearless Fonzie!"

"Yeah? What do I do? Jump out of the frying pan and into the fire?"

"It's a trick riding act," Madame LaZonga reported, reading the advertisement in the crystal ball. "You jump your motorcycle over the entire length of the sideshow."

"The fat lady included?" Fonzie asked, impressed.

"Even over the tallest man in the world."

"Is he on his stilts?"

"On his stilts and standing on a box!"

Fonzie frowned thoughtfully. "There's no doubt about it, that sounds like me," he said. "I don't know of anybody else who could do that if that guy is standing on a box."

"A *tall* box!" Madam LaZonga said.

"Let me get this straight," Fonzie said. "I am married to Lola, right? And I am doing a trick riding act in the carnival, right?"

"That's the future," Madame LaZonga replied. "You can't escape your fate. But—" She suddenly peered deeply into the crystal ball again. "Oh, my heavens!" she said delightedly. "Isn't this wonderful! It's what I've always wanted!"

"What? What? What?" Fonzie asked.

Madame LaZonga raised her eyes to him. "I'm going to be a grandmother!" she said ecstatically.

Fonzie snatched up the crystal ball. "How do you turn this this off!" he demanded.

"You can't! It's fate!"

"Ha! Ha Ha!" Fonzie said exultantly, looking into the crystal ball. "Is this the guy you're talking about, this guy on this bike?"

"That's you!" Madam LaZonga insisted. "It says 'Fearless Fonzie' on your jacket!"

"This guy on this bike with the black exhaust coming out the pipes?"

"With Lola, your loving wife, riding behind!"

Fonzie rolled the crystal ball across the table to her. "That's not me," he said confidently.

"It *is* you! It looks like you!"

"Sure, it looks like me," Fonzie admitted. "But it's not me, it's a ringer. That bike has got fouled plugs. No bike of mine ever had fouled plugs. See that exhaust? That exhaust is *dirty*. The Fonz don't ride on no bike with dirty exhaust."

"It's a borrowed bike!" Madame LaZonga charged. "Your own bike is in the shop for repairs."

"I don't jump over no fat lady on no borrowed bike!" Fonzie countered.

"It's you!" Madame LaZonga screeched. "Admit it—or my daughter will sue you for breach of promise!"

Fonzie looked at her levelly. "Heyyyy—I get it," he said. "Here's what's happened. Your daughter has got herself married to some guy who is on the lam. He's stole my jacket and he's using my name to hide his true identity!" He looked around again. "Where's the phone? I'm calling the cops!"

"No—wait!" Madame LaZonga said. Her manner softened. "Maybe the crystal ball was just doing some wishful thinking," she said. "It's been trying to get Lola married ever since the day she turned sixteen."

"Yeah, your crystal ball is a pushy mother," Fonzie said, moving toward the exit. "Okay. Don't forget the seance. And tell Lola I'll see her tonight—if I don't get waylaid by no carrots and celery." He paused at the opening. "And one other thing," he said, glancing back at the crystal ball. "Next time I see you, remind me not to ask you 'What's new?'"

SIX

Howard Cunningham arrived home early from the store the next day. As he stepped into the house, he became aware of an unusual quiet. Normally, there would be sounds of family activity. As Howard stood listening to the silence, mildly puzzled, the scent of something baking in the oven reached him. It was reassurance, telling him that he had not been deserted after all.

"Marion . . ." Howard called out, heading toward the kitchen.

"Oh, my!" There was alarm in Marion Cunningham's tone.

Howard reached the kitchen doorway and looked in. His wife was standing at the oven, with the door open. What Howard noticed first was that she was wearing a grass skirt. He next became conscious of a baffling incongruity. Along with the grass skirt she was wearing a checkered apron and a pair of oven mitts.

"Marion . . . what—"

"You're early!" she said accusingly.

"Of course I'm early. You told me we were having

an early dinner, because we're going to that seance this evening."

"That's right, I forgot. I mean, I didn't forget. But I for—" Tears came to her eyes. "I've done it all wrong."

"Done what all wrong?" Howard asked, entering the kitchen. "What are you doing in that grass skirt?"

"It's what you want, isn't it, Howard? A floozy in a grass skirt? Isn't that what you want? If that's what you want, that's what you were going to get." She sniffled. "I was going to meet you at the door in a grass skirt."

"Well, that's very romantic, Marion, but—"

"I know, but I look like an idiot," she said, "wearing oven mitts and an apron." Tears trickled down her cheeks. "I'm sorry, Howard, I'm just not a floozy. I tried." She sneezed. "But while I was putting on the grass skirt, I was thinking about dinner. The wife and mother in me just wouldn't let my family go hungry."

Howard smiled affectionately. "I'm glad, Marion," he told her. "I don't want to come home from work every night to a floozy in a grass skirt. The fact is, I have no interest at all in floozies—or anyone else—in grass skirts. What interests me—"

Marion sneezed again. And again and again.

"What interests me—" Howard began again, approaching her with a gleam in his eyes.

"How—" She sneezed once more—twice more—three more times.

Howard looked at her closely. "Your eyes are red, your nose is running and you're sneezing," he said.

"I know that, Howard. I feel awful," Marion said, closing the oven door. "And I so wanted to look sexy."

"Marion, do you remember why it is that we never have any dried flowers in the house?"

"Yes. Because they make my eyes red, my nose run, and make me sneeze."

Howard nodded. "And do you know what a grass skirt of made of?"

"Well ... grass?"

"*Dried* grass, Marion."

"Oh, my heavens! That's why my eyes are red, my nose is running and I'm sneezing. It isn't because I'm angry at myself for getting caught in oven mitts and an apron. It's because I'm wearing dried grass."

"That's *my* diagnosis," Howard said.

Frantically, Marion pulled off the oven mitts. She untied the apron strings, letting it drop. There was the rustle of dried grass.

"Marion—not here!" Howard said. "The children!"

"The children aren't here," Marion told him, rushing from the kitchen. "But, you're right, I can wait till I get upstairs."

She disappeared into the hallway.

Howard listened to the fading sound of sneezes, wincing at each one. When the sounds ceased, he smiled affectionately once more, then went to the oven and opened the door and looked in. What he saw, a roasting turkey, caused his smile to broaden. After a moment, he closed the oven door and left the kitchen and walked toward the front of the house. In the living room, he settled in his favorite chair with the afternoon paper.

Marion reappeared a short while later, dressed conventionally. Her eyes were still slightly red, but she was no longer sniffling or sneezing.

"Marion, will you get it out of your head that I'm going to run away with a hoochie-coochie dancer?" Howard said. "I like my life the way it is."

"Men are never satisfied," she said. "The grass is always greener on the other side—especially if it's a grass skirt."

"But I have the hardware store. No man in his right mind would give up a hardware store for— No, that's not the real reason," he said. He put the paper aside and got up and put his arms around his wife. "It's because I have you," he told her. "No man in his right mind would give up a wife like you for a hoochie-coochie dancer."

"That's sweet, Howard, but—"

"But what?"

"Remember what happened to your eyes when you saw all those hoochie-coochie dancers in one bunch? The same thing could happen to your mind. You could run away with a hoochie-coochie dancer without realizing what you were doing."

Howard smiled wryly. "I think I would know what I had in mind."

Marion blinked back tears.

"But it won't happen," Howard assured her. "And the reason is— The reason is . . . Marion, I love you."

"Oh, Howard . . ."

They kissed.

"Now, are you convinced?" Howard asked.

"Well . . . I suppose so," she said. "But I'd feel even more safe if you had the allergy to dried grass instead of me. The only thing I'm positive of is that I'll be glad when that carnival leaves town."

"So will I."

"Howard! Does that mean—"

"No! Marion, will you forget those hoochie-coochie dancers!"

From the direction of the front porch came sounds

of stumbling. Then the front door flew open and
Richie staggered into the house. He was followed by
Joanie, who was also having trouble staying on her
feet. They lurched across the living room, panting,
and collapsed on the sofa side by side. A moment
later Fonzie came strolling in. He was not even
breathing hard.

"What's the matter with them?" Howard asked
Fonzie, indicating his son and daughter. "What happened?"

"Don't race your motor," Fonzie replied. "Nothing
is wrong. Everything's okay. We been out running,
that's all. I'm in training for the fight, see, and the
running is to get me in shape. Not that I need it."

Marion looked at Richie and Joanie, stretched out
exhaustedly, then faced Fonzie again. "If you've all
been running, why are they perspiring and gasping
for breath," she asked, "and you're not?"

"The Fonz does not perspire," he explained. "The
Fonz does not gasp. Perspiring and gasping is not
cool."

Richie tried to speak, but failed.

"How do you do that, run and not perspire?"
Howard asked Fonzie, amazed.

"It's a simple matter of mind over sweat," Fonzie
replied. "You got to make up your mind who is in
control of your destiny, you or your sweat glands."

"Water!" Richie gasped.

"Just open your mouth," Fonzie told him. "You got
enough water pouring down your face to fill a swim-
ming pool and have enough left over to do a wash."

"I'll get you a drink, dear," Marion said, hurrying
from the room. "You, too, Joanie."

Howard bent over Joanie. "Are you all right, sweetheart?"

Panting, she nodded.

"Actually, you look better than you have for days," Howard told her. "Your color is coming back. It came a little too far back, in fact. But I suppose it will settle down to normal when you get your breath."

"Yeah, are you over your sick?" Fonzie asked Joanie. "How did it work out?"

Joanie managed to speak. "It was ... it was ... it was a total ... a total failure," she anwered. "I got sick for nothing."

"You're still a girl?"

She nodded.

"Maybe you're.lucky," Fonzie said. "As sick as you looked there for a while, you could have gone right past being a woman and turned into an old lady."

Marion returned with two glasses of water. "Just sip," she advised, handing the glasses to Richie and Joanie.

Fonzie sniffed the air. "Hey! Is it Thanksgiving?" he said.

"No, but it *is* a turkey—and all the trimmings," Marion told him. She turned to Howard. "I thought if the grass skirt didn't work a big meal might," she said.

"Hey, turkey—that's my favorite chicken!" Fonzie said. "And stuffing?"

She nodded. "And sweet potatoes and cranberry sauce."

"One of my favorite feelings is being stuffed with stuffing," Fonzie said.

"Fonz ..." Richie said, finally able to speak. "Fonz ... you're in training, remember."

"Yeah? So?"

"You can't stuff yourself," Richie said. "You've got to eat well, but intelligently." He addressed his mother. "Small portions for Fonz," he said.

"Hold it!" Fonzie said. "Look, Cunningham, I don't mind this training as long as you're the one who's doing the suffering, sweating and out of breath. But when it comes to you telling me how much I can eat of my favorite chicken, that's when I call a halt. Didn't you ever hear? The way to the world's heavyweight championship is through a man's stomach."

"That's 'The way to man's heart is through his stomach'," Marion told him. "It was said by a woman whose grass skirt failed her."

"Fonz, overeating turns muscle into fat," Richie said. "You don't want to go into the ring flabby, do you?"

"Flabby? Me? It couldn't be. It's not The Fonz. I got a corpuscle inside me that, anytime any flab gets near me, it flattens it out with a hammer."

"Who told you that?" Howard asked

"Nobody told me. I figured it out myself. The flattened flab turns into brain matter. That's how come I'm so smart and can figure things out like that."

"The theory makes sense," Howard conceded.

"So, it's turkey and all the trimmings for The Fonz," Fonzie said.

Richie shook his head. "Fonz, you've got a responsibility to all those people who are betting on you," he said. "You've *got* to stay in training. And that means, some of everything, but *small* portions."

"The less I eat, the stronger I get, huh?"

"Well, not exactly. You see—"

"That's what it sounds like to me," Fonzie said. "So,

I'll tell you what I'm gonna do, Cunningham. I am going to become the strongest human being on earth. I am not going to eat anything." He strode from the room. "From this minute on, The Fonz is on a fast!"

The room was silent for a moment after he had gone.

"Do you think he really means it?" Marion wondered.

"He might," Howard said. "He seemed pretty angry."

"Nah, he'll get hungry and that will be the end of the fast," Richie said. "I hope," he added nervously.

"Once Fonzie makes up his mind, it's made up," Joanie said.

"Yes, and if he sticks to the fast and loses his strength, the Mauler will maul him," Howard said. He frowned worriedly. "I wish now that I hadn't bet that fifty cents on the fight."

"Fifty cents!" Marion said. "Howard, is that all the faith you have in Fonzie?"

He looked penitent. "You're right, Marian—that isn't much faith. Tomorrow I'll put down another fifty cents on him."

"Maybe you better not, if he's going to fast," Richie said.

"I think I know how to end the fast," Marion said. "I'll put dinner on the table. When the aroma reaches Fonzie's room," she said, departing for the kitchen, "I'm sure he'll decide that he's starved himself long enough."

"Your mother is a very wise woman," Howard told Richie and Joanie when Marion had gone.

"But Fonzie can be awfully stubborn," Richie said.

From the direction of the kitchen came a cry of alarm from Marion. "Fire!"

Howard rushed into the hallway and Richie and Joanie leaped up from the couch and followed. A few seconds later, they arrived in the kitchen. Marion was standing in front of the open oven.

"Where's the fire?" Howard asked excitedly, looking around.

"There isn't any fire," Marion replied.

"But you yelled 'Fire'!"

"It was the first thing that came to mind," she explained. She pointed to the oven. "It's gone!"

"Marion, the oven isn't gone. It's right—"

"The turkey!" she told him. "The turkey is gone! We've been robbed!"

Howard laughed. "Marion, who ever heard of anybody stealing a turkey? It isn't stolen, it's just mislaid. Where did you have it last?"

"In the oven! It's been in the oven all afternoon! Why would I take it out? What do you think I've been doing, carrying it around the house with me while I did the dusting?"

"You don't think—" Richie began. He shook his head. "No, he wouldn't."

"Of course he wouldn't," Howard said. "Still—"

There was a sudden rush for the doorway. With Howard in the lead, the Cunninghams raced from the kitchen and up the stairs When they reached Fonzie's room, Howard pounded on the door.

"Ain't nobody here—including no chickens," Fonzie answered from inside.

Howard threw open the door and the Cunninghams plunged into the room. Fonzie was stretched out on his bed with a wide, happy smile on his face. On the table was a platter. And on the platter was the carcass of a turkey, stripped to the bone.

"Our dinner!" Marion moaned.

"Can you identify it?" Fonzie challenged. "I don't see no turkey fingerprints around." He suddenly winced. "Oh!"

"That's what you get for overeating!" Richie said. "Indigestion!"

"That's not indigestion, Cunningham," Fonzie replied, content again. "That was that corpuscle taking a swing at a flab with its hammer. It missed and hit a rib."

"Well," Marion said, glancing toward the platter, "evidently you left the trimmings. We can still have sweet potatoes and cranberry sauce for dinner."

"That's not much of a meal," Howard said. "What about a main course?"

"Try a stalk of baked celery," Fonzie suggested "I'm told it's *very* healthy."

It was early evening when the Cunninghams and Fonzie and Potsie and Ralph arrived at the gate of the Addams' mansion for the seance. Richie rang the bell.

"This place looks like a palace," Howard said, peering through the gate. "Old Addams must have been a bigger crook than I thought."

"Maybe he was just very frugal and saved his pennies," Marion said.

"No, he gave his pennies away as tips to waiters," Richie told her.

"That explains it," Howard said. "If I still had all the money I've given away in tips to waiters, I could buy—" He frowned thoughtfully. "Well, I might be able to buy a pup tent."

"Howard, we don't have a pup," Marion said.

"That was just a way of comparing—"

Howard interrupted himself. "Someone is coming," he said, squinting into the dimness.

The butler appeared. "You can't *all* be working your way through college," he said crisply to the group standing outside the gate.

"No, we're not selling magazines," Richie said. "We're here for the seance."

The butler began unlocking the gate. "I knew the fat one couldn't be a freshman," he said.

"Chubby! Chubby!" Howard responded indignantly.

"He could have meant me," Fonzie said soothingly to Howard. "Maybe the turkey is showing."

The butler led them along a walkway and into the mansion. The foyer was almost as large as the entire Cunningham house, with marble pillars and elaborate chandeliers and walls hung with huge paintings.

"Hellooooo!" Fonzie called out.

The echo came back. "Hellooooo!"

"Who's the greatest, The Fonz?" Fonzie called out.

The answer came back, reverberating. "The Fonzzzzz . . . The Fonzzzz . . . The Fonzzzz . . ."

"When even a house knows it, there's no argument," Fonzie said.

"Folow me, please," the butler said, moving on. "Mrs. Addams and those persons are in the library."

"Lola and the witch are here already, I guess," Fonzie said. "They're awful eager. I never heard of anybody who was doing somebody a favor being early. Or even showing up on time. What's in it for them?"

"Maybe Madame LaZonga charges for her seances," Howard said.

"No, she said it's for free," Fonzie replied. "And it'll probably be worth every penny of it."

They entered an enormous room that was lighted only by candles. The walls were lined with shelves that were crammed with books. There was a large table in the center of the room. Seated at one end was Madame LaZonga. Lola was closing the drapes at one of the two tall windows. Mrs. Addams was standing by, looking fretful.

"The other persons," the butler said, announcing the Cunninghams and Fonzie and Potsie and Ralph.

"You're late," Madame LaZonga said testily.

"How can we be late?" Fonzie replied. "Nothing starts until The Fonz shows up."

Richie introduced his parents and sister to Madame LaZonga and Lola and Mrs. Addams, then introduced Mrs. Addams to Fonzie.

"Any word yet from your hubby?" Fonzie asked her.

"Maybe I'm just imagining," she replied, "but I *do* believe I sense his presence. I've been on pins and needles all evening. I just know he's coming back to scold me for something. When he was still alive, you know, the only time he spoke to me was when he had a complaint."

"You don't have to take that off him any more," Fonzie told her. "If you don't like what he say when he comes back, tell him to shove off. The money's in your name now, isn't it?"

"Why ... I never thought of that. But, yes, that's true."

"Threaten him with a candle," Fonzie suggested.

"Those ghosts are all the same, they're afraid their sheets will catch fire."

"Chester Addams is not a ghost," Madame LaZonga said. "He is a spirit. He doesn't wear a sheet."

"Oh, my, no sheet?" Marion said. She turned to Joanie. "You better wait out in the foyer, dear."

"No, no, no, we won't see him," Madame LaZonga said. "We'll only hear him. He'll speak to us through me, the medium."

"It's time, Mother," Lola said.

"Let's all sit down at the table," Madam LaZonga said. "Lola, get the lights, please."

Lola began snuffing out the candles.

"Hey, no sense wasting all this good darkness," Fonzie said to Lola. "They can sit at the table and you and me will find a corner someplace."

"I've got to leave one candle burning," she replied.

"And I need everyone at the table," Madame LaZonga told Fonzie. "But you and Lola can use our tent later if you want to talk in private. We don't have any candles there."

"This scene must be getting to me," Fonzie replied to the fortuneteller. "What you just said made sense."

When they were all seated at the' table—except Lola, who was standing by the single lighted candle—Madame LaZonga placed her hands on the top, palms down, and closed her eyes.

"It's getting creepy," Joanie whispered.

"Quiet!" Madame LaZonga commanded. "I must have absolute quiet!"

Mrs. Addams began murmuring softly.

"Shhhh!" Lola said.

"I'm just reminding myself that the money is in my name," Mrs. Addams explained. "I just know Chester is going to scold me about the donations I've made to charity since he passed away. He always said that if charities wanted money they ought to get it the same way everybody else does, by cheating on their income tax returns."

"Quiet, please!" Madame LaZonga pleaded.

The room became silent.

Madam LaZonga's hands began to twitch gently. "Chester Addams is in this room," she announced. Then abruptly her body became stiff, as if she had gone into shock.

"Here comes Chester," Fonzie said. "He did the same thing to her last time. I think he sneaks up behind her and konks her over the noggin."

"That's a trance," Lola said. "If Chester is here, he'll speak to us . . . any second now . . ."

Madame LaZonga's lips moved. She spoke—but in a voice that was deep and gruff, as if she had a frog in her throat.

"Who turned out the lights?" the voice complained.

"Chester!" Mrs. Addams responded. "It's you!"

"Who the devil did you think?" Chester replied, still speaking through Madame LaZonga.

"Chester, how are you?" Mrs. Addams asked brightly.

"Terrible, terrible," Chester replied. "As long as this place has been around, they still don't have air conditioning. It's a hundred-and-ten in the shade, night and day. Order a cold drink, and the ice cubes are melted before you can get the first sip."

"Oh, my," Mrs. Addams said. "I haven't ever heard Heaven described that way before."

"I'm not in Heaven, drat it. I'm down here with all the other income tax cheaters."

"Well, at least you have someone to talk business with," Mrs. Addams said consolingly. "Chester, why have you come back? If it's an air conditioning unit you want, I don't know how I can get it to you. Does Railway Express deliver there?"

"No. The joker in charge wouldn't let me keep it, anyway," Chester replied. "He claims that heat is good for the soul."

"How?"

"By being bad for the soul. I tell you, everything all balled-up down here. In Milwaukee, if you had horns and a tail, you'd be a freak. Down here, you're normal. A guy showed up here last week with wings and a ring of light over his head and scared the daylights out of everybody. They thought he had a terrible disease."

"Poor thing," Mrs. Addams said. "I hope he isn't being snubbed."

"No. He didn't belong here, as it turned out. He took a wrong turn just east of purgatory. But he's gone now . . . most of him."

"Most of him?"

"One of the boys swiped his ring of light," Chester explained. "We roll it around like a hoop. It passes the time."

"Chester, if it isn't air conditioning you want, why did you come back?" Mrs. Addams asked. "But, before you answer that, I just want you to know that the money is in my name now. So don't scold me or I'll get after you with a— Oh . . . where you are, I suppose you wouldn't be frightened by a little thing like a candle."

"Here, a candle burn is a reward," Chester told her. "It's what we get when we've been bad."

"But you said it's a reward."

"That's what we get rewarded for, drat it, being bad."

"Chester, you're confusing me," Mrs. Addams said edgily. "Will you please tell me why you came back?"

"For money," Chester replied. "Why else would I travel all that distance—not to mention the bad roads between purgatory and Chicago."

"Money?" Mrs. Addams said, perplexed. "But, Chester, haven't they told you? You can't take it with you."

"The devil you can't," Chester replied. "That's a lie. It's propaganda put out by the bankers! They want to keep that cash in their banks, so they can loan it out and charge interest. I'm the only one down here who fell for that line. Everybody else is loaded!"

"Ohhhh . . . poor Chester . . ."

"Hey, hold it!" Fonzie said. "Hey, Chester, if everybody up there is loaded, what do they do with all that dough?"

"Who's that?" Chester asked.

"It's me, The Fonz," Fonzie replied. "Answer the question, will you?"

"We play poker," Chester replied. "We don't have the energy to do anything else. This heat is murder."

"Chester, if that's what you want the money for, I'm not going to send it," Mrs. Addams said. "Gambling is evil."

"It's too late for that," Chester told her. "I've been sitting in on the game ever since the first day I got here. Jack the Ripper is holding my I.O.U.s for five thousand smackers. That's what I need the money for, to buy back those I.O.U.s."

"Yeah, what if you *don't* buy them back?" Fonzie asked.

"They won't let me roll the hoop any more," Chester replied.

"All right, Chester, I'll send you the five thousand dollars—but on one condition," Mrs. Addams said. "You must promise me that you'll stop gambling."

"Sure, I promise. A promise doesn't mean a thing down here."

"How will I get the money to you, Chester?"

"By osmosis," he replied. "You hand the cash over to Madame LaZonga and I'll osmosis it from her to me."

"I'm not sure that I understand—"

"You just get the mazuma," Chester said, "I'll worry about the details."

"All right ... Is there anything else, Chester?"

"Oh, make that five thousand and one dollars," Chester said. "There's a fifty-cent toll charge for the boat across the Styx River, and I owe them for both ways, coming and going."

"But won't you need some spending money, too?" Mrs. Addams asked.

"No, from now on I'm going to be the big winner in that poker game," Chester told her.

"How can you be so sure?"

"I made a deal with the guy in charge down here," Chester explained. "I traded him my soul for an eternity's worth of good luck."

"But, Chester—if you're down there, you must have sold him your soul years ago."

"Sure. But he doesn't know that," Chester said. "I told you he's a joker. He keeps lousy books."

Madame LaZonga suddenly emerged from the trance.

"Chester!" Mrs. Addams called out. "The five thousand—big bills or small?"

"Too late, he's gone . . . back to the beyond," Madame LaZonga told her. "But make that big bills. They're easier to osmose." She turned to Lola. "We can have some light now, dear," she said.

"That was an exhilarating experience!" Mrs. Addams said.

"Weird," Fonzie agreed. "Are you sure that was your late husband talking to you?" he asked her.

"Well, back to the carnival," Madame LaZonga said quickly, rising. "Things to do, fortunes to tell! Busy, busy, busy!" She addressed Mrs. Addams. "When can you have the money?" she asked.

"Tomorrow, I suppose."

"Unfortunately, Chester can't come back that soon," Madam LaZonga said. "Travel is so tiring on the spirits."

"Yeah, those rough roads between purgatory and Chicago," Fonzie said.

"Saturday night," Madame LaZonga said. "I'm sure Chester will be rested by then."

"Hey, isn't that the last night the carnival is in town?" Fonzie said.

"Why, yes, by pure coincidence, I believe it is," Madame LaZonga replied.

"That's the night of your fight, too, Fonz," Richie said.

"The coincidences have coincidences on their coincidences," Fonzie commented. "Everything happens just before the carnival pulls up stakes and lams it out of town. It's almost like it was planned that way."

"Do something!" Madame LaZonga said to her daughter.

Lola grabbed Fonzie by the hand and pulled him toward the doorway. "I saw a garden!" she said. "Let's go for a walk in the moonlight!"

"Excuse us, all," Fonzie said to the others, allowing Lola to tug him along. "I got an urgent appointment to make a deal on my soul."

SEVEN

It was lunch hour when Fonzie, Richie, Potsie and Ralph arrived at the local gym. Consequently, they had the premises almost to themselves.

"Look—everybody else is somewhere eating lunch," Fonzie said. "That's where I should be. I need food. I can't keep going on that turkey forever."

"First the workout, then the food," Richie told him. He indicated the wicker basket he was carrying. "I have all the fresh vegetables you can eat in here."

"Right now, one nibble off a carrot is all the fresh vegetables I can eat," Fonzie said. "I'm hungry for food, not roots and grass. What am I, a forest creature?"

Ralph cackled. "That's good, Fonz—a forest creature."

"Shud-dup."

"I'm shutting, I'm shutting," Ralph assured him, backing away.

"All right, Fonz," Richie said, "we'll make a deal. Give us about an hour's workout. Then we'll go to Arnold's and you can have a hamburger ... maybe two ..."

97

Fonzie looked around at the facilities. "What've you got in mind for a workout?"

"Some rope-skipping, weight-lifting, bag-punching," Richie replied.

"How about one hamburger before and one hamburger after?" Fonzie countered.

"Fonz," Potsie said, "you know what will happen if we go to Arnold's now for a hamburger, before the workout. We'll never get you back here. We'll blink our eyes or something, and you'll be gone."

"I can hear it now—the roar of the motorcycle," Richie said to Fonzie.

Fonzie looked at them innocently. "Do I detect a hint of untrustedness?"

"You sure do," Richie replied. "We're not going to let you out of our sight until this workout is over."

Fonzie shrugged resignedly. "Okay. I'm stuck." He addressed Ralph. "Hand me a weight."

Ralph walked over to the collection of barbells and bent over to pick one up. He did not straighten.

"Okay, okay, let's have it," Fonzie said impatiently.

"I can't lift it," Ralph replied, still bent over.

"You are about as useful as an oar in a submarine," Fonzie said, going to him. He picked up Ralph and set him aside, so that he could get at the barbell. But Ralph retained his grasp on the weight and it went along with him. Fonzie dropped them both. "I don't mind lifting the barbells," he said to Richie. "But if I got to pick up your friends, too, I got to have a hamburger first."

"Ralph, get out of the way and let Fonzie work, will you?" Richie said.

Ralph straightened. "Did you see that!" he said, flabbergasted. "I couldn't even lift the barbell and

Fonzie not only picked up the barbell, but me along with it!"

"It was a snap," Fonzie told him. "Counting what you got in your head, you don't weigh much." He picked up the weight and easily raised it over his head, then put it down. "So much for that," he said. "What next?"

"Fonz, that isn't much lifting."

"One lift is just like another," Fonzie replied.

"I know, but—"

"What I'm telling you is, if you've done it once, you've done it a thousand times," Fonzie said. "Are you telling me a thousand lifts is not enough?"

"That's a *lot*, Richie," Ralph said. "I couldn't even do it once."

"All right, let's go on to rope-skipping," Richie said.

"Heyyyyy! Rope-skipping! That is for kids!" Fonzie said.

"It strengthens the legs," Richie told him. "If you're going to go ten rounds with the Muskogee Mauler, you'll need strong legs."

"In that case," Fonzie said, "we can skip the skipping. I don't intend to go any ten rounds with the Mauler. My plan is to drop him in round number one—round number two, maybe, if my timing is a little off."

"In that case, you better practice your punching," Richie said, escorting Fonzie to the punching bag. "Face it, Fonz, you're not going to get out of here until you finish your workout."

Fonzie studied the bag. "You want me to give it the punch that I'm going to give the Mauler, right?"

"Right."

Fonzie pulled back a fist and let it go. It hit the

bag and the bag went sailing across the gym and flying out an open window.

"Awwww ... look what I did," Fonzie said. "Now, I got to go out and get the bag and bring it back before I can do any more workout."

"Oh, no!" Richie said quickly. "I'll go get the bag. I know what will happen if you leave here. You won't come back."

"The roar of the motorcycle," Potsie said, agreeing with Richie.

"You guys are too smart for me," Fonzie said. "Okay, Cunningham, you go get the bag. While you're gone, I'll do some more working out on the weights. Tweedle-dumb-dumb and tweedle-dumb-dumb," he said, indicating Ralph and Potsie, "can stay here and watch me so I don't vamoose."

"He won't get away from us, Rich," Ralph said.

"If he vamooses, we'll stay right with him, nagging him," Potsie said.

With some misgivings, Richie left the gym and walked around to the rear of the building in search of the punching bag. He found it immediately. It was in the arms of a small boy.

"That belongs inside," Richie said.

The small boy shook his head. "It's mine," he said.

"No, it's a punching bag, it came out the window."

"It's a giant egg," the small boy said. "A giant bird dropped it and I caught it."

"Punching bag."

"Giant egg."

"Look at it," Richie said. "It leather."

The small boy nodded. "A giant leather bird dropped it," he said.

Richie reached for the bag.

The small boy screamed. "Help! Murder!"

"Shh-shh-shh!" Richie said. "I'm not murdering you. All I want is that punching bag."

"It's a valuable giant leather egg," the small boy insisted.

Richie pondered for a second. "How valuable?" he asked.

"A dime?"

"It looks like about a five-cent giant leather egg to me," Richie said.

"A quarter?" the small boy countered.

"A dime."

The small boy held out a hand. "Feed the palm," he said.

Richie gave him a dime and received the punching bag in return, then headed back toward the gym.

The boy called after him. "I can sell you some giant leather bacon to go with it!"

Richie ignored the offer.

Entering the gym, Richie found Potsie and Ralph flat on their backs on the floor, held down by a pair of heavy barbells. Fonzie was nowhere in sight.

"Where is he!" Richie asked.

"You just missed him," Ralph replied. "He handed us these weights, then walked out. Maybe you can still catch him!"

From outside came the roar of a motorcycle engine.

"Too late!" Potsie said.

"Richie, take these barbells off us," Ralph said.

"Just a second," Richie replied. "I've got to hang up this giant leather egg."

Arriving at the carnival grounds, Fonzie parked his

bike, then walked on to Madame LaZonga's tent. Lola and her mother were there.

"Hey—it's the bad witch of the north and the good witch of the west—or whatever," Fonzie said amiably, entering the tent.

Lola giggled coyly.

But Madame LaZonga glared. "Lola, find something to do and somewhere else to do it," she said to her daughter. "I want to talk to Mr. Fonzarelli alone."

"All right, Mother," Lola replied obediently, departing.

"What's this?" Fonzie asked Madame LaZonga. "It sounds like the beginning of a conversation where the father hauls out a shotgun and points it at the boyfriend and tells him he's got a choice between a load of buckshot and a ceremony at the church altar."

"That's it," Madame LaZonga told him.

"What's your grounds?" Fonzie asked.

"That's what I want to know," she replied. "What happened in that garden at the Addams house the other night?"

"Oh, that ..." Fonzie said vaguely. He backed toward the exit. "I just remembered: I haven't had lunch. I never talk about gardens on an empty stomach."

"Sit down!" Madame LaZonga ordered. "I have some cake and I'll make you some tea. And we'll talk."

"Tea? Tea?" Fonzie said. "Do I look like a tea drinker?"

"I'll lace it with a little beer," Madame LaZonga offered.

"A little beer, a little cake, who could refuse," Fonzie said, sitting down at the table.

Madame LaZonga put water on to heat for tea. "What happened in that garden?" she asked again.

"What did Lola say happened?"

"She was delirious."

"Yeah, well, I was a little delirious myself," Fonzie said. "And, at first, I couldn't figure it out. Because nothing happened to make anybody delirious. It was like a mysterious spiritual happening."

"Applesauce!" Madame LaZonga said, getting out the cake.

"No thanks, not with beer," Fonzie said.

"I mean applesauce to a mysterious spiritual happening," Madam LaZonga said. "I was young once myself, you know." She began cutting into the cake.

"Forget about the slices, just bring over the whole thing," Fonzie said. "And, you're right, as it turned out, it wasn't a mysterious spritual happening."

"In other words, I have grounds," Madame LaZonga said, putting the cake on the table in front of him.

"In other words, no," Fonzie replied. "I thought about it and thought about it and finally figured it out. What happened in that garden was, we was attacked by a bed of snapdragons."

Madame LaZonga looked at him doubtfully.

"I got the snapdragon bites to prove it," Fonzie said.

Madame LaZonga sighed defeatedly. "I suppose that *could* induce delirium," she said, returning to where the water was heating. "However," she said, "I still want to discuss your intentions. Lola is a very sweet girl."

"The snapdragons thought so," Fonzie said, breaking off a piece of cake.

"And she adores you," Madame LaZonga said.

"What female in her right mind don't?" Fonzie responded.

Madame LaZonga returned with a cup of tea and placed it in front of Fonzie. "She'll make a wonderful wife," she said. "Perfect for you," she added. "She's the kind of cook who would serve tea laced with beer."

Fonzie sipped the tea. "It tastes funny," he said.

"Do you suppose it's the beer?"

"It must be," Fonzie decided. "I never tasted beer with junk in it before—unless you count pretzel crumbs as junk."

"Is it Lola, or are you just afraid to get married?" Madame LaZonga asked.

"Afraid? 'Afraid' is not the word," Fonzie told her. He sipped the tea again. "This is the funniest funny taste I ever tasted."

"If 'afraid' isn't the word, what is the word?" Madame LaZonga persisted.

"'Brains' is the word," Fonzie told her. "Look, I am The Fonz. Nothing can change that. I was born The Fonz and I will still be The Fonz when everybody else dies and leaves me the only human being left on earth. That is a great responsibility. But don't think it's all a bed of roses. There are some snapdragons to it, too. My life isn't my own. I'm like Superman, somebody's always in a jam that I got to get them out of. What kind of life would that be for a wife? She puts the dinner on the table and I got to jump up and leap on my bike and ride off and get somebody out of a jam. A marriage like that wouldn't even last through the honeymoon. I'd have to go rescue some nerd who was going over Niagra Falls in a barrel or something."

He broke off another piece of cake. "That's what I mean when I say the word is 'brains'."

Lola reappeared. "Now?" she asked.

"Now," Madame LaZonga replied drearily. "Talking to him is like trying to read a fortune in a bowling ball."

"I won the conversation, didn't I?" Fonzie said. He smiled. "Brains," he confirmed.

"I surrender," Madame LaZonga said. "I won't ever bring up the subject of marriage again." She addressed Lola. "Just stay away from snapdragons," she said.

Fonzie sipped again. "That's not a beer taste," he said.

"It's tea," Lola told him.

"Your old lady slipped in a little beer."

"Beer? We don't—"

"Leftover beer!" Madam LaZonga said, interrupting her daughter. "Leftover beer from the bottle at the back of the refrigerator."

Lola's eyes widened. "Oh! Oh ... *that* leftover beer!"

"Hey! Now I know what this taste reminds me of," Fonzie said. "When I was a kid, I got caught in some quicksand in a swamp. Luckily, there was a tree limb overhead and I pulled myself out. But while I was pulling I lost my shoes and socks in that quicksand. That's what this taste tastes like."

"Quicksand?" Lola asked.

"No, those socks, after they been rotting out there in that swamp all these years," Fonzie replied.

"There's a piece in the paper about the fight—Fonzie and the Muskogee Mauler," Howard said to

Richie and Joanie that evening as they sat in the living room waiting for dinner to be announced.

"What does it say?" Richie asked.

"In general," Howard replied, "it says that if Fonzie doesn't win, Milwaukee will never be able to hold its head up again. I think that's a slight exaggeration."

"I guess it won't be that bad," Richie said. "But it will be pretty awful. If Fonzie loses, the whole town will be broke."

Howard lowered the paper. "Has that much money been bet on him?"

"That's what I hear," Richie replied.

Howard thought for a moment. "I've got fifty cents on the fight myself," he said. "Considering how close I am with a buck, that must mean that that fight promoter is into this town for thousands upon thousands."

"If Fonzie loses," Joanie said, "it will be a financial disaster!"

"Well ... a half-buck isn't *that* much," Howard said.

Marion called in, "Dinner everybody!"

Howard and Joanie and Richie left the living room and went into the dining room.

"Where is Arthur?" Marion asked, as they were sitting down at the table.

"He wasn't with us," Richie replied. "He must be up in his room," he said, leaving. "I'll get him."

Richie climbed the stairs and knocked on the door to Fonzie's room.

"Cunningham?" Fonziie replied.

"Yeah, Fonz, it's me. Dinner is ready."

"Cunningham, are you alone?"

"Sure."

"Come in!" Fonzie said, sounding urgent.

Puzzled, Richie opened the door and looked in. Fonzie was nowhere in sight.

Fonzie's voice came from out of nowhere. "Close the door."

Richie obeyed. "Where are you?" he asked, baffled.

"Look under the bed!"

Richie went to the bed and got down on his hands and knees. "Fonz! What are you doing under there?"

"Cunningham, you are looking at a shadow of The Fonz's former self," Fonzie replied from under the bed. "From now on, you can call me The Znof. I am backwards from what I was!"

"Fonzie, I don't understand what you're talking about," Richie said.

"Picture this: I come home from the garage, where I been giving a Chevy a grease job, and I come up to my room. Got it?"

Richie nodded.

"Now, nobody can give a grease job without getting a little grease under his fingernails, not even The Fonz," Fonzie continued. "I got a very delicate touch, but, even so, a little grease cannot be avoided."

"I understand, Fonz. But what are you getting at?"

"To clean the grease out from under my fingernails, I pick up, as I usually do, a toothpick," Fonzie said. "That is when I first notice the change. Cunningham, that toothpick was no cinch to pick up."

Richie laughed. "Cut it out, Fonz."

"I'm serious. But, anyway, I proceed, as normal, to clean the grease from under my fingernails. Again, I notice that something is not quite right."

"What now?" Richie asked.

"The grease seems heavier than usual."

"Fonz, is this a joke?"

"I wish it was. Wait'll you hear what happens next. I finish cleaning out the grease—and it's no easy job—and then, the way I always do, I start to break the toothpick in two."

Richie stared at him.

"It's not cool to use a toothpick twice, Cunningham," Fonzie said. "A lot of nerds will do it, but not The Fonz. After I use a toothpick once, I break it in two and throw it away. Okay?"

Richie nodded again.

"Only, this time, I can't do it!"

"Can't do what, Fonz?"

"I can't break the toothpick! I haven't got the strength! I am like Superman without his phone booth!"

Richie smiled thinly. "That's funny, Fonz," he said. "But, look, dinner is ready. Want to come down and eat?"

"Cunningham, don't talk food at me! I'm telling you the truth—I couldn't break the toothpick! I tried and I tried again. I am an overweight ninety-pound weakling! Me—The Fonz! Check that! Me—The Znof."

Richie studied him a moment, still not wholly convinced. "Is this something like the knock-knock jokes, only new? Toothpick jokes? he asked.

"Cunningham, if I had the strength, I would throw you out of this room and up the hall and down the stairs."

"Okay, okay, I believe you," Richie said. "But . . . but maybe it's the toothpick. Maybe it was made out of especially strong wood or something."

"It's over there on the table," Fonzie said.

Richie got up and went to the table and picked up the toothpick. As he started to bend it, it snapped, breaking cleanly in two.

"Did I hear what I think I heard?" Fonzie called out from under the bed.

"I'm afraid so. I broke it."

"Then throw it away so no nerd will use it again."

Richie dropped the two halves of the toothpick into the waste basket, then went back to the bed and got down on his hands and knees again. "What I don't understand is what you're doing under there," he said.

"This is where I live from now on," Fonzie told him. "I can't go walking around on the streets when I'm not myself. Somebody will come up to me and say 'Hey, Fonz!' and I won't know who they're talking to."

"Fonz, it's probably only temporary. You'll get your strength back."

"Who are you, a doctor?"

Richie brightened. "That's what you need, a doctor," he said.

Fonzie sighed glumly. "It couldn't hurt," he said. "I got a feeling it won't help . . . but it couldn't hurt . . ."

Richie jumped up. "I'll get you a doctor!" he said, hurrying from the room.

"Get me two doctors! One for The Fonz and one for The Znof!"

When Richie reached the dining room he told the rest of the family what had happened to Fonzie. The story was met with disbelief.

"He wants to get us up there to his room," Joanie said, "then he's going to lock us in and come down here and eat our whole dinner himself."

"Honest—he's lost his strength," Richie said. "We've got to get a doctor."

"I wonder if it has anything to do with the fight?" Howard said. "Could it be that he's pretending to have lost his strength because he's afraid to fight the Mauler?"

"Dad, that's not Fonzie," Richie said.

"Well, you told me he's claiming to be somebody called the Znof."

"I believe you, dear," Marion said. "I'll call a doctor." She left the room.

"I want to see this overweight ninety-pound weakling," Howard said, heading for the stairs.

When Howard, Richie and Joanie entered Fonzie's room a few moments later, Fonzie was still in hiding under the bed. They all got down on their hands and knees.

"I feel like a monkey in a cage, all you tourists looking in at me," Fonzie complained.

"Are you sure you're not trying to make monkeys out of us?" Howard asked. "Fonzie, how could you possibly lose your strength? It's not something you carry around with you in your pocket, like a wallet."

"Or roast in an oven like a turkey," Marion said, joining them. "I called a doctor," she reported. "He's on his way."

"Have you been anywhere near Mom and Pop Mauler?" Richie asked Fonzie. "I bet they put a whammy on you so you'll lose the fight."

"I haven't seen them since the last time," Fonzie told him.

"Besides, there's no such thing as a whammy," Howard said. "Unless, of course, you happen to believe in the whammy. Do you?" he asked Fonzie.

"I believe in the whammy like I believe in the Easter Bunny," Fonzie replied.

"Is that yes or no?"

"What do you mean, is it yes or no?" Fonzie replied crossly. "The Easter Bunny is like Santa Claus, it's your old man dressed up in a red suit."

From downstairs came the sound of knocking at the front door.

"The doctor!" Marion said. "I'll let him in."

"If this is a joke," Howard said to Fonzie, when Marion had gone, "this is your last chance to pull the punch line. The doctor will know if you've lost your strength or not."

"I am so weak I couldn't pull a punch line if I had one," Fonzie replied. "I am so weak, the line would get in the first punch."

"Fonz . . ." Richie said hesitantly. "You're not afraid of the Muskogee Mauler, are you?"

"Cunningham, handsome I am, and brilliant I am, too, but stupid I'm not. Of course I'm afraid of the Mauler! In my condition, I'm afraid of an ant! I could get trampled before I could get out of the way!"

Marion returned, accompanied by the doctor, an elderly man with feathery white hair and thick glasses. She introduced him as Dr. Switzel.

"Oh, all you need is to lose a few pounds," the doctor said to Howard. "Carrying around all that weight, that's what saps your strength."

"I am not the patient," Howard replied testily. "The patient is under the bed."

"You'll have to haul him out," Dr. Switzel said. "Most doctors don't even make house calls any more. None of us crawls under beds."

With Marion's and Joanie's coaxing and Howard's

and Richie's pulling, Fonzie was lured and dragged from his hiding place and seated upright on the bed.

"Looks fine to me," Dr. Switzel said, delivering a preliminary opinion.

Fonzie held out two fingers. "I am so weak, I can't cross them," he said.

"There isn't a lot of call for that, anyway, I wouldn't imagine," the doctor said. "Why don't you get a new vocation?"

"That's not my job! It's what I can't do."

The doctor reached out and crossed Fonzie's two fingers. "There you are," he said. "That will be five dollars."

"Where did you get this nerd," Fonzie asked Marion, "out of some medical school trash can? They must've thrown him out with the used bandages!"

"Doctor," Howard said, "the trouble is that Fon-zie—"

"Fonzie?" Doctor Switzel interrupted. "The Fonz? Is this The Fonz?"

"Yes. He—"

"The Fonz who is fighting the Muskogee Mauler?"

"Yes. And he's lost his strength—he claims."

"Great heavens!" the doctor said, appalled. "And I have a quarter bet on the fight!" He made shooing motions. "Everybody out of the room! I've got to make a thorough examination. Not you," he said to Fonzie. "You stay. I'll need you for the examination."

The Cunninghams stepped out into the hall and the door closed behind them.

"Howard, I'm worried," Marion said. "I don't think Arthur is pretending. I think he's really as weak he says he is."

"I'm beginning to be convinced, too," Howard said. "I hope it's not some rare disease."

"If it is, we'll take care of him," Marion said, her eyes becoming moist. "We'll nurse him back to health. We'll wait on him hand and foot, night and day, week in and week out, month after month, year after—"

"And sell the screen rights to our story of unselfish devotion for a million dollars," Howard said, interrupting. "Marion, let's wait until we find out what the doctor has to say before we dedicate our lives to nursing Fonzie back to health."

"I wonder if Fonzie will ever be able to ride his bike again," Richie said.

"If he can get it under the bed, why not?" Howard replied.

"I think it's psychological," Joanie said.

"And why exactly do you think that, Dr. Freud?" Howard asked.

"Because it's just like a movie I saw last week on television," she explained. "Except that the patient was a mountain climber who was afraid to climb Mount Everest."

"Afraid why, dear?" Marion asked.

"He had a premonition that he was going to fall off."

"Oh, my!"

"What happened?" Richie asked.

"The psychiatrist cured him," Joanie said. "He showed the mountain climber that Mount Everest was really his fanatical ambition to succeed and that he was afraid to climb it because he was afraid of failing."

"That's beautiful," Marion said, her eyes filling with

tears again. "And the mountain climber, cured, climbed the mountain!"

"Yes," Joanie replied.

"I love happy endings," Marion said.

"It wasn't a happy ending," Joan said. "He fell off."

"Oh ..." Marion dried her eyes. "Well, it's the thought that counts," she said.

"But what has the movie got to do with Fonzie?" Howard asked Joanie.

"Don't you see? It's so obvious. Just like the mountain climber, Fonzie has a psychological problem."

"Joanie, what I'm getting at—"

The door opened. Dr. Switzel motioned the Cunninghams back into the room. When they entered, Fonzie was still sitting on the edge of the bed, looking as glum as before.

"A perfect specimen of manhood!" Dr. Switzel announced to the Cunninghams, beaming happily on Fonzie. "I have never seen a man before who was in such perfect physical condition, I think my two-bit bet is safe."

"He has his strength back?" Marion said.

"Strong as an ox!" Dr. Switzel said. "Except that he can't uncross his fingers."

"But—" Howard began.

Dr. Switzel raised a hand, interrupting. "But I prescribed for that," he said.

"Oh."

"I told him to keep his hand in his pocket. Nobody will notice his crossed fingers. I had another case once almost exactly like this," he said, "a man who lost one of his ears. I told him to wear his hat at a tilt."

"Will you get this quack out of here!" Fonzie said. "Before the room is overrun with duck hunters!"

"Doctor, I don't think keeping his hand in his pocket is really the solution," Howard said. "Isn't there anything you can do about his loss of strength?"

"There isn't anything I can do about it because he hasn't lost his strength," Dr. Switzel replied. "I told you: he's a perfect physical specimen, as strong as an ox."

"Then why can't he uncross his fingers?"

"It's all in the head," the doctor replied.

"Psychological!" Joanie said.

"If you want to be technical, yes," Dr. Switzel replied. "I call it 'all in the head'. Or, if it's a bad case, I call it 'the crazies' or 'the loonies'."

"Then he needs a psychiatrist," Howard said.

"Yes," the doctor said, heading for the door, "but you'll have to wait until morning. Psychiatrists not only don't make house calls or crawl under beds, they don't see patients after the sun goes down and the moon comes up."

"Why not?" Marion asked.

The doctor paused in the doorway. "Because when the moon comes up," he said, speaking secretively, "they all turn into werewolves!"

EIGHT

The entire Cunningham family escorted Fonzie to the office of the psychiatrist, Dr. Piltzer, the next morning. They arrived just as the doctor, a tall, curly-haired, amiable-looking young man, was unlocking his office door.

"I'm a little late this morning," Dr. Piltzer said, apologizing. "Hard time getting up this morning." He winked. "I had a hairy night last night."

"Hey! They *do* turn into werewolves!" Fonzie said.

Dr. Piltzer chuckled. "That's an old wives tale," he said. "The old wives see us running around, all furry and baying at the moon, and they tell everybody." He gestured the family and Fonzie into his outer office. "Well, which one of you is the cuckoo?"

"None of us is cuckoo," Howard replied. He indicated Fonzie. "But this one may have a psychological problem. He claims to have lost his strength—"

"Claims!" Fonzie said. "A toothpick is stronger than me."

"Have you had a physical exam?" Dr. Piltzer asked him.

Howard answered. "He's had a physical exam and the doctor says he's in perfect condition."

"Hmmmm," Dr. Piltzer said. "A toothpick is stronger than he is, yet the doctor says he's in perfect condition. I think you brought me the wrong patient. I ought to be seeing that doctor."

"No, the doctor says his loss of strength is all in his head," Marion explained.

"Weak mind, eh?" He addressed Fonzie again. "Take two aspirin, get plenty of rest and— No, that's for me, for my hangover. Is strength important to you?" he asked Fonzie. "Maybe you're better off without it. Nobody will ever ask you to open a stuck jar lid again."

"He needs his strength," Richie said. "This is The Fonz. He's fighting the Muskogee Mauler tomorrow night."

"*The* The Fonz!" Dr. Piltzer said. "You're right, this is a serious problem. I have bet on that fight." He frowned thoughtfully, studying Fonzie closely. "This is a textbook case," he said finally. "To you," he told Fonzie, "The Muskogee Mauler is not just another fighter, he's Mount Everest. You're afraid that if you try to climb him, you'll fall off. And," he said sadly, "if the chap who wrote the script for that picture on television the other night knows anything about psychiatry, you're right—you *will* fall off."

"Get me out of here!" Fonzie said to the Cunninghams. "If I wasn't a loony before, another couple minutes with *this* nerd and I will be!"

Dr. Piltzer took him by the arm and led him toward the inner office. "Nobody cheats me out of my fee," he said. "You're going to be cured whether you want it or not. I see your problem. Your ego is in conflict with your id."

"What's my ego? What's my id?" Fonzie asked, puzzled.

"I've never been completely sure," Dr. Piltzer replied. "I have a strong suspicion that id stands for 'identification card'. And I think ego is just egg spelled wrong."

The door closed behind them.

"I'm afraid I don't have much faith in him," Marion said. "Wrong is spelled w-r-o-n-g."

The door to the inner office opened and Dr. Piltzer reappeared, trembling. "Get that maniac out of here!" he demanded. "I can't treat him!"

"What did he do?" Howard asked.

"He's hiding under my couch! I have an intense fear of people who hide under couches!"

"That's silly," Marion said. "People who hide under couches can't hurt you."

"I know! I know!" the doctor said. "But when I was a small child my mother used to hide under the couch. We couldn't afford a play pen for me, so hiding under the couch was the only way she could get away from me for a while. I understand her motivation—she just wanted a few minutes of peace and quiet. But, even so, anytime anyone hides under a couch in my presence, I suffer intense rejection feelings."

"We'll get him out," Howard said. He motioned to Richie and they entered the inner office.

"Otherwise, I'm perfectly normal," Dr. Piltzer told Marion and Joanie. He lowered his voice. "For instance, I know that your friend Fonzie hasn't really lost his strength. It's a ruse. He just wanted an excuse to come here and hide under my couch!"

"Why would he want to do a thing like that?" Marion asked.

"He's one of *them*," the doctor replied. "They've organized—it's the 'Get Dr. Piltzer Club'. They take turns coming in here, using any old excuse, and hiding under my couch." He lowered his voice even more, almost to a whisper. "My mother is their leader," he revealed, trembling again.

Howard and Richie came out of the inner office with Fonzie between them.

"Out!" Dr. Piltzer shouted. "And tell my mother I give up, she wins! I'll get in my play pen and I'll never come out!" He fled into the inner office and the door slammed behind him.

"I'm no psychiatrist," Fonzie said, "but I know what that guy's trouble is. When that mountain climber fell off Mount Everest in that movie the other night, he landed on Piltzer's brains."

When the Cunninghams reached home, Howard and Richie helped Fonzie up to his room. He immediately disappeared under the bed again.

"Fonz, you can't stay under there!" Richie said.

"Cunningham, I *got* to stay under here—until I get my strength back," Fonzie replied. "For a guy who can't even break a toothpick in two, the world is a dangerous place. I'm not under here because I'm a coward, I'm under here because I'm smart."

"I don't think I understand that."

"How many guys would you say there are in this town who have stepped out of line and The Fonz has had to put the scare into them?"

"Hundreds. Thousands, I guess."

"And what is going to happen when those guys find out that The Fonz is so weak he can't even break a toothpick?"

"I see what you mean . . ."

"Right. They are going to start lining up for the chance to break The Fonz in two like a toothpick. So, the smart thing for The Fonz to do is to stay under here until his strength comes back."

From below came the sound of knocking at the door.

"Maybe that's another doctor," Richie said. "You need help, Fonz. I don't think hiding under a bed is a cure for loss of strength."

"No more doctors! One doctor examines me and tells me I'm crazy, and the next doctor I go to turns out to be crazier than I am. I tell you, Cunningham, it's a dangerous place out there in the outside world. The next doctor could be a surgeon and he'd probably want to amputate me from the neck down to keep the craziness in my head from spreading to my toes! The only smart thing for me to do is to stay right here, where the doctors can't get at me."

JoJo the Dog-Faced Boy appeared in the doorway.

"Hi," Richie said.

"Your mother told me I could come up," JoJo said. "I'm looking for Fonzie."

Richie pointed under the bed.

JoJo got down on his hands and knees. "Mrs. Cunningham told me what happened to you," he said. "I'm sorry. Is there anything I can do?"

"Yeah, don't bring me any doctors," Fonzie replied. "I think that's what I need most."

"I just came to tell you that, thanks to you, I've finally found the courage to leave the carnival," JoJo said. "I'm going to become a sculptor."

"Yeah ... well, maybe you better think it over a little more," Fonzie replied. "It's a dangerous world out there, you know."

JoJo looked stunned. "But you told me I ought to 'do', not think," he said.

"There's a wise old saying," Fonzie replied. "It goes 'Never do today what you can put off until it's too late to do it, anyway'. You got a pretty good life at that carnival, you know. You get paid regular, and all you got to do is sit around with a collar on and maybe run and fetch a stick every once in a while."

"But—"

"Think about all the dangerous things that could happen to you in the outside world," Fonzie said. "There are doctors out there just waiting to amputate your head off to save your toes. And that's just one example. For another, a mountain climber could fall off Mount Everest and land on your brains. That's happened! I saw the horrible result personally. The victim that got landed on is so loony, they have to keep him caged up in a play pen. Not to mention his mother."

"Fonz—" Richie began.

"Let me set this guy straight, Cunningham."

"But, Fonz, this isn't you talking," Richie said. "You're not afraid of life. You've just been hiding under that bed too long. Come out."

"That's another thing," Fonzie said to JoJo. "If you leave the carnival, take your bed with you. You'll need it to hide under."

JoJo looked terrified. "I— I— I don't think I'll be leaving the carnival after all," he said.

"Smart," Fonzie said. "And, listen, if I was you, I'd ask the carnival owner to get me at tag to hang on my collar. What if you got lost? Nobody would know where you belonged. They might take you to the pound."

JoJo leaped up. "I've got to get back to my tent!" he cried, fleeing. "The dogcatcher is after me!"

"I probably saved his life," Fonzie said, when JoJo had gone. "He didn't realize what terrible dangers are lurking out there in the outside world."

"Fonz, if anything, you ruined his life," Richie said sadly. "You're not yourself anymore. Will you please come out from under there? Where is the *old* Fonz? The Fonz who wasn't ever afraid of anything?"

"Yeah, I guess I'm letting this temporary muscular weakness get to me," Fonzie replied. "For all I know, maybe it's gone away already. Hey—hand me a toothpick."

Richie rose and got a toothpick from the table, then crouched again and passed the toothpick to Fonzie.

Fonzie gripped it at the two ends. "Ready for the snap, Cunningham?"

"I'm ready. Make it good and loud."

Fonzie strained, exerting all the strength he had on the ends of the toothpick. Nothing happened.

"You still ready for the snap, Cunningham? Here it comes! Any second now!"

"I'm ready, Fonz."

Fonzie strained again. The toothpick refused to break—or even bend.

"Cunningham, I think you gave me an iron toothpick. Hand me one of the old-fashioned wooden ones."

"That's a regular toothpick, Fonz."

"Close the window," Fonzie said. "I think there's a draft in here. I always have trouble with toothpicks in a draft."

"There's no draft, Fonz."

Fonze handed the toothpick back to him. "And you want me to come out of hiding! The only way I will come out from under here before I get my strength back is if I have a bodyguard to protect me. Cunningham, don't you see?" he said. "I am at the mercy of any guy who wants to make a reputation for himself. I am The Fonz. Nobody beats The Fonz—the *old* Fonz. But, the way I am now, all some guy would have to do to beat me would be to breathe on me hard. Then I wouldn't be the Fonz any more, *he* would be The Fonz."

"Where is he?" a voice said from the doorway.

Richie looked up. Potsie and Ralph were standing in the doorway.

"We just heard," Ralph said. "Your mother told us. Is it true? Has Fonzie lost his strength?"

Richie nodded.

Ralph bounded into the room and began shadow boxing. "Where is he?" he said. "Where are you, Fonz? Come out, come out, wherever you are!" He delivered a right, then a left to an imaginary opponent. "I, Ralph, challenge The Fonz!"

"What did I tell you?" Fonzie said to Richie. "I knew that as soon as the news got out, some nerd would be after me. Little did I know that it would be the king of the nerds himself."

"Ralph, will you stop it," Richie said.

Ralph lowered his fists. "Aw, come on, Rich," he said. "This is my chance to meet a lot of girls."

"What girls?"

Potsie explained. "He thinks if he beats Fonzie all the girls will want to know him," he said. "I told him it's a crazy idea. What will happen when he wins is that the girls will decide that they like losers better. The Fonz will still have the girls."

"But, after I beat him, I'll be The Fonz," Ralph said.

"Anybody else, maybe," Fonzie said from under the bed. "But not you. You will still be The Nerd."

Ralph struck a fighting pose. "Come out of hiding and say that!" he challenged.

There was silence for a second.

Then Fonzie spoke. "That is the medicine I needed—a nerd calling me out," he said. "Okay, Tweedle-dumb-dumb, I am coming out!"

Ralph panicked, racing for the door. "I didn't mean it, Fonz!" he cried, disappearing through the opening. "It wasn't me talking! I was drunk with nerdness!"

"Come back!" Fonzie called, emerging from under the bed.

After a second, Ralph peeked around the frame of the doorway. "Don't kill me, Fonz! My mother would never forgive you. My mother *likes* me!"

"There is no accounting for tastes, as the old lady said when she kissed the cow," Fonzie replied. "Anyway, you don't have to worry about me killing you. I need you." He sat down on the edge of the bed. "I got to go to that seance tonight at the Addams Place," he said. "And, until I get my strength back, anytime I leave this room, I got to have bodyguards. You and Potsie and Cunningham, you're my bodyguards."

"You *need* me?" Ralph said, overwhelmed by the honor.

"Yeah. Then, after I don't need you no more, I'll kill you. But first things first."

"Why do you have to go to the seance, Fonz?" Richie asked.

"A little suspicion I got in my mind," Fonzie replied.

"What?"

"You know how when Chester comes back from the beyond, you can hear him talking but you can't see him?"

"Yeah?"

"When you can hear it but you can't see it," Fonzie replied, "believe me, there is more to it than meets the eye."

Richie, Potsie and Ralph were standing close to Fonzie, watching for attackers, when they arrived at the Addams mansion that night, along with Richie's parents and Joanie.

"Not *that* close!" Fonzie said to Ralph, as Richie rang the bell at the gate. "If you get any closer, you'll be on the other side of me."

"I'm sorry, Fonz," Ralph said. "How close do you want me to be?"

"Close enough so that I know you're there, but not so close so that I'm all the time reminded of it," Fonzie replied.

Ralph took a step away. "How is this?"

"About twenty-thousand-and-two more steps, that'll be about right," Fonzie replied.

"That would take me almost to Lake Michigan."

"Your calculation is off," Fonzie told him. "It would put you a half-mile out in Lake Michigan, in the deep part."

The butler arrived. "Well, if it isn't the other persons again," he said, with obvious distaste. "Here to pick up last month's magazines for the College Dropouts Club paper drive, are you?"

"When I get my strength back, he is going to be the third nerd to get it," Fonzie said. "Right after those two quacks, Switzel and Piltzer."

"We're here for another seance," Howard told the butler. "Has Madame LaZonga arrived yet?"

"If she hasn't," the butler replied, unlocking the gate, "then Hansel's and Gretel's witch has escaped from the oven and is in the library with Mrs. Addams."

When they were inside the grounds, the butler led them into the house and through the foyer, down a corridor and into the library. Lola was waiting just inside the entrance. Her mother and Mrs. Addams were seated at the long table. Mrs. Addams was nervously counting thousand-dollar bills, while Madame LaZonga watched her avariciously.

"You look terrible!" Lola said immediately to Fonzie. "I just *know* something's happened. Hasn't it?"

"He lost his strength," Ralph told her. "He's as weak as a newborn puppy. Weaker even. He can't even break a toothpick in two. He's so weak, you could knock him over with a feather. If he gets in the ring with the Muskogee Mauler and the Mauler takes a deep breath, Fonzie will go right down his windpipe. He's had the best doctors, but they've given up on the case. He'll probably be this way the rest of his life ... although nobody knows how long that will be. Richie and Potsie and I are protecting him, but, you know how things happen. One of these days, we'll let our guard down and somebody will get past us and get at

him. Poor Fonz. After that, somebody else will be
The Fonz. Fonz will be somebody named Joe or
Frank—or even Cyril, maybe. But, we'll all remember
him and the good old days when he was ... when he
was ... whatever his name was ..."

"The mouth strikes again," Fonzie said disgustedly.

"Did I say something wrong?" Ralph asked innocently.

Fonzie did not have the opportunity to reply. He
found himself wrapped smotheringly in Lola's arms.

"I'll take care of you, dear," she told him. "You
won't ever have to break another toothpick again. I'll
be there to do it for you!"

"Heyyyy! That's a load off my mind!" Fonzie replied. "Only let up a little on the taking care of me,
you're choking me."

Lola released her hold on him. "I'll be by your
side—forever!" she told him.

Madame LaZonga called over. "The minute we
leave here, we'll go straight to the owner of the carnival" she said happily.

"What's he gonna do?" Fonzie asked.

"He's like the captain of a ship," Madame LaZonga
explained. "He can perform marriages."

"Please!" Mrs. Addams said crankily. "You're making me lose count." She began again. "One ... two ...
four ... five ... six ... I did it again! There are only
supposed to be five here."

"Why don't you let Chester worry about that," Fonzie suggested. "Where he is, he probably expects to
get short-changed, anyway."

"Why, that's true!" Mrs. Addams said, brightening.
"Anyway, I'm sure there's five thousand dollars here.
The bank teller counted it before he gave it to me.

Oh ... I must remember ... When I told the teller what I wanted it for, he asked me to say hello to Chester for him ... and to tell him that he would be seeing him soon."

"I wonder how he knows that," Potsie said.

"The teller has the idea that all bankers go where Chester is," Mrs. Addams explained. "He says it started when some money-changers in a temple somewhere had some trouble with a long-haired radical, and, ever since, it's a cross that bankers have had to bear. Frankly, I didn't understand any of it. I was watching him count the money. How *did* he do that?" she said, starting a new count of the thousand-dollar bills. "One ... two ..."

"Ten to one she blows it again," Fonzie said.

". . . two . . ." Mrs. Addams said once more, counting the third bill.

"I'll take ten-cents' worth of that bet," Howard said to Fonzie.

". . . eleven . . ." Mrs. Addams said, counting the fourth bill.

"Hark!" Madame LaZonga said suddenly.

"Chester must have smelled the money," Fonzie said. "I think he's on the way."

"Lola—the candles!" Madame LaZonga ordered. "Everyone else—sit at the table!"

Taking Fonzie's hand, Lola tugged him along with her. "You need me now," she told him. "We've got to stay close together."

"I'll say one thing: you're an improvement over my last bodyguards," Fonzie replied.

By the time Lola had pinched out the flames on all of the candles save one, the others were seated around the table. She took up a position behind her mother's chair, keeping Fonzie close beside her.

Madame LaZonga placed her hands flat on the table and closed her eyes. "Chester ... Chester ... Chester ..." she said. "Can you hear me?"

"You better use his full name," Fonzie advised. "Some *other* Chester is liable to slip in here and grab off those five big ones."

"That cat we had named Chester would do that," Potsie said. "He would take anything. He was a regular pack rat. My father said that was why he was always chasing his tail. It was the cat in him after the rat in him."

"Quiet!" Madame LaZonga said. "Chester is—"

She suddenly became stiff.

"I once knew a guy that did the same thing on one bottle of beer," Fonzie said.

Madame LaZonga's lips moved, and the voice of Chester Adams was heard. "Get out! Scat!" he shouted. "They were calling me, not you!"

There was a loud meowrrrrrr!

"Dratted cat!" Chester complained. "He followed me all the way from Chicago!"

"Chester!" Mrs. Addams called out.

"Hello! Hello! Nice to talk to you again. Where's the money?"

"I have it right here! Five thousand dollars—eleven one-thousand-dollar bills! How do— Oh, and the teller at the bank said to say hello to you and that he'll be seeing you soon."

"He sure will," Chester replied. "They're all down here. The place is overrun with bank tellers and motorcycle riders who don't marry until late in life."

"Hold it!" Fonzie said. "I think I smell a rat!"

"That's that cat. He's chasing his tail again," Chester said.

"Chester, how do I get the money to you?" Mrs. Addams asked.

"I told you that the last time. Just give it to Madame LaZonga and I'll osmosis it through the what'sit from her to me."

"Through the what, Chester?"

"The what'sit," he replied irritably. "That stuff that separates your world from our world. It's like fog. We get it from a guy who does special effects for horror movies. The joker who's in charge down here buys it used. The problem with that is, it sometimes still has monsters and actors wandering around in it. We had Godzilla and Bela Lugosi both with us for a whole week last month."

"Chester . . . that's a little hard to believe . . ."

"I don't know why. Their agents are permanent residents," Chester said. "Are you going to give me that money or do I have to send the cat after it?"

"Well, all right . . ."

Mrs. Addams put the five one-thousand-dollar bills in Madame LaZonga's outstretched hand.

"One for the money," Chester said, "two for the show. Three to make ready and four to—Go!"

Madame LaZonga, her eyes still closed, began thrashing her arms about, with the result that it was impossible for the others to keep her hands in sight.

"The last time I saw this," Fonzie commented, "it was done with three shells and one pea."

Madame LaZonga's hands disappeared below the table, then immediately reappeared. The one-thousand-dollar bills were gone.

"I got it!" Chester called out.

The stiffness went out of Madame LaZonga's body. "It's all over!" she announced.

"Mother, it's not," Lola said tightly.

"Yes, it is, dear—it's all over," Madame LaZonga said.

"Mother, it's *not!*" Lola insisted, becoming panicky. "It's *not* over—understand?"

Madame LaZonga stared at her. "You mean it's not over?"

"What is going on here?" Howard asked.

"Nobody move!" Madame LaZonga said. She began looking around on the floor near her chair. "There's been a slip-up. Chester didn't get the money!"

"But we heard him tell us that he had it," Mrs. Addams said.

"That was the cat talking," Madame LaZonga said, scrambling around on the floor. "I tell you, Chester did *not* get the money."

"She's right," Fonzie said. "The one the money was intended for did not get it."

Madame LaZonga stopped scrambling and looked up at him warily. "Chester wants to take that back about motorcycle riders who marry late in life," she said.

"Tell Chester it's too late."

"Chester says he's willing to split, fifty-fifty," Madame LaZonga said.

"Tell Chester he's talking to the wrong cat this time," Fonzie advised her.

"Chester says—" Lola began.

"Not that, either," Fonzie said, interrupting.

"If this is a game," Potsie said, "let's make it Simon says. I know that one."

"The game is over," Fonzie announced. He raised a

hand—and in it were the five one-thousand-dollar bills. He handed them back to Mrs. Addams. "Chester's loss is your gain," he told her.

"I— I don't understand."

"It is what is called the fast shuffle," Fonzie told her. "Your husband Chester was never here, not in body nor soul nor voice. That was Madame LaZonga doing the talking for him. Also, the meowrrrring for the cat."

"Why, I never!" Madame LaZonga said, outraged.

"On the contrary, you *always*," Fonzie said. "I bet you pull this swindle in every town you hit. You look through the back-date newspapers and get the name of somebody rich that died, then you arrange to meet up with the deceased's leftovers."

"Survivors, I think you mean," Howard said.

"Whatever. In this case, she used Richie to put her in touch with Mrs. Addams. And when Mrs. Addams agreed to the seance, Madame LaZonga was home free—almost."

"But how did you get the money, Fonz?" Richie asked.

"By a sheer stroke of unsleight of hand," he replied. "What Madame LaZonga does, see, once she gets hold of the cash, is wave her arms around so nobody can see what's going on. Then, all of a sudden, when she's got everybody's eyes confused, she reaches behind her and hands the cash to her daughter."

"Who just happens to be standing behind her chair," Howard said.

"Right. Only, this time, not only was Lola standing behind Madame LaZonga's chair, but The Fonz was too. Imagine my surprise when somebody all of a sudden shoves a handful of crisp cash into my mitt!"

"Darn!" Ralph said.

"What's the matter with you, Tweedle-dumb-dumb?"

"That wasn't how I guessed how it happened," Ralph replied. "I thought Godzilla got the money, then passed it back to you through the what'sit."

Fonzie shrugged. "Well, maybe that's the way it happened. Either way, the money is back where it belongs."

Mrs. Addams glared at Madame LaZonga. "You un-nice woman!" she said.

"Where is the phone?" Howard asked Mrs. Addams. "I'm going to call the police."

"No—don't do that!" Madame LaZonga said. "I'll do it for you!" She grabbed Lola by the hand and rushed toward the door, pulling her daughter after her. "It's no trouble!" she called back. "I saw a phone booth up the road! I'll telephone the police from there!"

Then Madame LaZonga and Lola were gone.

"Well, she turned out to be rather nice after all," Mrs. Addams said. "Not many people would call the police to have themselves arrested. I suppose I owe her an apology for what I said."

"Yeah, next time you see her, you tell her that," Fonzie said.

"Well, as someone is always bound to say in a situation like this, all's well that ends well," Marion said.

"Only it's not the end and it's not so good," Fonzie said. "I still got a fight with the Muskogee Mauler. And there is still a big hunk of cash bet on me. And I still don't have my strength back."

"Are you sure it's not back, Fonz?" Richie asked.

"May I?" Fonzie said to Mrs. Addams, picking up one of the thousand-dollar bills.

"Of course. You deserve a reward."

"No, I don't want to keep it, I just want to try to bend it."

"Chester had a little quirk like that, too," Mrs. Addams said. "He liked to run through a room full of thousand-dollar bills barefoot."

"This is no quirk," Fonzie said. "This is the test. Am I The Fonz, or am I The Znof?"

As the others watched tensely, Fonzie got hold of the thousand-dollar bill by the two ends, then exerted his full strength in an effort to bend it. It remained stiff and straight.

"I'm The Znof!" Fonzie said drearily.

"No, wait, Fonz!" Ralph said. "That's a thousand-dollar bill! No wonder you can't bend it. Try something smaller—a ten or a five or a one." He dug into his pocket. "Better yet, try this—a nickel!"

NINE

When Howard arrived home from the store on the night for which the fight was scheduled, he had the feeling that he was reliving a disturbing experience. The house was silent, as if it were deserted. He hurried directly to the kitchen, expecting to find Marion dressed in a grass skirt and apron again. But he found no one there.

"Hello!" Howard called, making his way back toward the front of the house. "Anybody home?"

Marion answered. "Up here, Howard."

When he reached the stairs, she was standing at the second-floor landing.

"We're all in Fonzie's room," she said. "He's still weak. Some of us want him to stay and fight and some of us want him to leave town." She smiled softly. "I'm glad to see you, dear," she said. "I wasn't sure that you'd come home. Today was the day of the Booster Club luncheon, wasn't it?"

"Today was the day," Howard replied unenthusiastically, climbing the stairs.

"Were the hoochie-coochie dancers there?"

"They were there, Marion . . . I think."

"Don't you know?" she asked puzzledly.

Howard halted. "Marion, Dr. Fenton Wilson is a boring lecturer. When he is explaining that the tarsus bone is connected to the fibula bone, and the fibula bone is connected to the tibia bone, and so on and so on, it just doesn't matter how the bones are dressed or what they're doing. Impossible as it may seem, he made those hoochie-coochie dancers in grass skirts look like fleshless skeletons—in the mind's eye, that is."

"Oh, Howard, I'm so glad!"

"Well, we learned our lesson at the Boosters Club," Howard said. "We fired me as entertainment and education committee chairman." He joined Marion and they walked toward Fonzie's room. "Is he hiding under the bed again?" he asked.

"No. He's packing and unpacking."

"I won't ask you to explain that. After that lecture on anatomy, I don't want anything else explained to me for another six months."

When they reached Fonzie's room, Fonzie was piling clothes into a suitcase that was open on his bed. He was surrounded by Richie, Potsie, Ralph and Joanie.

"But, Fonz, if you run out, with all that money bet on you, you'll never be able to come back," Richie said.

"You're right," Fonzie replied. "I got to stay." He began taking the clothing from the suitcase.

"But, Fonzie, if you get into the ring with the Muskogee Mauler the way you are, weak, he might cripple you for life!" Joanie said.

"You're right!" Fonzie said, tossing the clothing back into the suitcase. "I got to get out of here!"

"I see what you mean about packing and unpacking," Howard said to Marion. "He's going to wear those clothes out, putting them in and taking them out."

"But, Fonz," Richie said, "your weakness is all in your head. If you just—"

"Hold it!" Fonzie said. "I don't like the way you said that, Cunningham."

"Your lack of strength is psychological, I mean."

"That's better. But it's wrong. My weakness is in my muscles. My head is in tip-top condition. I know, because my head is telling me that if I get in the ring with the Mauler the way I am, I'll have something wrong with my head." He began packing again.

"Fonzie," Potsie said, "this isn't like you. You're not thinking about all those guys who bet all that money on you."

"That's exactly what I'm doing, thinking of them," Fonzie said. "If I'm not here, there can't be any fight. And if there isn't any fight, all bets are off. They'll get their money back."

"You know what everybody will say, though, Fonz," Ralph said. "They'll say you were chicken."

Fonzie looked at him levelly. "When you say 'everybody' will say that, who does that everybody include?"

"Not me, not me!" Ralph replied quickly. "I know you're not chicken, Fonz. Look—" He flapped his arms and cackled. "—I'm the one who's chicken!"

"On the other hand," Fonzie said, addressing the entire group again, "if I stay and fight—in my condition—I will lose. And, that way, the guys who bet on me will lose right along with me. So," he said, resuming the packing once more, "the best thing for everybody is for me to get out af town."

From downstairs came the sound of knocking at the front door.

"I think that's either the cavalry or the Marines," Howard said. "This is the spot where one or the other of them usually comes to the rescue."

"I hope they're not planning to stay for dinner," Marion said, departing to answer the knock. "We're having potluck."

"But, Fonz, think about yourself," Richie said, continuing the debate. "Ralph is right, if you run out on the fight, everybody will think you were scared. Think how it will be when you come back. You won't be The Fonz any more."

"Yeah ... well, maybe I won't come back," Fonzie said. "Maybe I'll just get on my bike and keep going."

"I guess it would be a great chance to see the world," Potsie said.

"You got that backwards," Fonzie said. "It's a great chance to let the world see me."

Marion returned. "It's your friend, Mr. Boy," she said to Fonzie. She was accompanied by JoJo the Dog-Faced Boy.

"I know what's wrong with you!" JoJo told Fonzie. "I should have realized it when I was here before, but I was only thinking about myself. You've been doped!" he said.

"Mom Mauler did it, I bet!" Richie said.

"No, Madame LaZonga did it," JoJo said. "Did she give you something to drink?" he asked Fonzie.

"A little tea, laced with a little beer," Fonzie replied. "It was the funniest-tasting tea and beer I ever tasted. But I didn't think a lot about it, since I hadn't ever tasted tea and beer together before. I kind of expected it to taste a little bit funny."

"That wasn't beer," JoJo said. "It was dope. She's used it before. It clouds men's minds."

"I hope it's not rain clouds," Fonzie said. "I don't want any thunderstorm going off in my head."

JoJo got a small bottle from his pocket. "I brought the antidote," he announced. "She keeps it in the back of the refrigerator, right next to the dope. I sneaked into her tent while she and Lola were out and got it." He handed the bottle to Fonzie. "Drink this!"

"Wait a minute," Fonzie said. "I don't go around putting a lot of unknown things in my stomach. I stick to regular food, like beer and hamburgers." He opened the bottle and sniffed. "What is this? It smells like glue."

"I don't know what it is. It's the antidote, that's all I know," JoJo replied. "Look at the label."

Fonzie held the bottle up. "Yeah, it says 'Antidote' on it. Hold it here's something else. 'Also for pasting pictures in the family album,' it says."

"What I don't understand," Howard said, "is why Madame LaZonga would want to dope you. So you'd lose the fight, is that the reason?"

"I think she had something more in mind than that," Fonzie replied. "Basically, I guess, she's just like every other mother. She wanted The Fonz for her son-in-law. And the only way to get me married to Lola, she figured, was to cloud my mind."

"Then Dr. Switzel was right," Richie said. "Physically, you're as strong as you ever were. Your weakness is in your mind."

"Cunningham, you did it again."

"Sorry, Fonz. I mean, your problem is psychological."

"Wrong again," Fonzie said. "My problem is that dope." He raised the bottle. "Here's to a clear head," he said. He drank, emptying the bottle. "Cunningham, hand me a toothpick."

"One thing—" JoJo began.

"Just a minute," Fonzie said, accepting the toothpick that Richie was handing to him. "I want to celebrate my comeback."

Fonzie gripped the toothpick by the two ends, then exerted his full strength. The toothpick did not even bend.

"That's what I was going to tell you," JoJo said. "It takes time for the antidote to work."

Fonzie groaned. "How *much* time?"

"I think it depends," JoJo replied.

"On what?"

"On how much time it takes."

"You know what you ought to be?" Fonzie said to him. "You ought to be a doctor." He tossed the toothpick aside. "Okay—what I got to do now is wait." He began packing again. "And, if I'm as smart as I think I am, I'll do the waiting in Pittsburgh or San Luis Obispo or someplace, where the Muskogee Mauler can't get at me."

"Fonz, you can't run! Not now!" Richie protested. "Not with your strength coming back!"

"How do I know my strength is coming back? For all I know, the only thing I'll ever be good for any more is pasting pictures in the family album."

"You've got to take JoJo's word for it! You've got to trust him!" Richie said.

Fonzie looked at JoJo.

JoJo looked away. "You don't have any reason to trust me," he said.

Fonzie hesitated.

Ralph spoke. "You ought to trust him, Fonz," he said. "He's man's best friend."

Fonzie glared at Ralph, then addressed JoJo. "I trust you because you're *my* friend," he said. "If you say my strength will come back, that's all I need to know." He began unpacking. "I'm staying," he announced. "The fight is on!"

TEN

The Mauler's tent was jam-packed with fight fans and a cheer went up as Fonzie entered that night, accompanied by the Cunninghams and Potsie and Ralph. Responding to the cheering, Fonzie raised his hands over his head, signifying his confidence.

"Don't encourage them, Fonz," Ralph said, keeping his voice low. "Remember, you still can't break a toothpick in two."

"What am I supposed to do?"

"Hedge," Ralph suggested. "Just hold one hand over your head."

When they finally managed to make their way through the crowd to ringside, they found Mom Mauler there.

"I hope you've got a hearse parked outside," Mom Mauler said to Fonzie. "When you leave here, you'll be going straight to the cemetery."

Fonzie looked into the empty ring. "Where is Sonny?" he asked. "Loading his gloves with horseshoes?"

Mom Mauler cackled. "He's going to let you go the

first round alone," she told Fonzie. "That's the only way you'll stay on your feet."

The crowd suddenly erupted in boos and catcalls. The Muskogee Mauler was entering the tent, following by Pop Mauler.

"Here's my baby!" Mom Mauler shouted. "Kill, Sonny, kill!"

As the Mauler and Pop Mauler climbed into the ring, Fonzie got out of his shirt. When he was bare to the waist, Richie handed him a toothpick. Fonzie gripped it at both ends and strained. The toothpick remained as straight as a toothpick.

"Fonz, I've changed my mind," Richie said. "You better get out of town!"

"Now, you tell me that!"

In the ring, the Mauler was snorting and flexing his muscles.

"Don't let him scare you, Fonz," Potsie said. "Just remember, it won't last long. He'll probably hit you once and that will be it."

Fonzie turned to Ralph. "I guess you got something to say to build up my confidence, too," he said.

"Just 'Goodbye', Fonz," Ralph replied. "And it's been nice knowing you. Oh ... and one other thing— Have you left a will? If not, now's the time to do it. And if you want to leave your bike to me—"

Fonzie grabbed him by the collar.

"Fonz! The antidote is working!" Richie said. "Look! You're almost bending the material!"

Fonzie released his hold on Ralph. "I got a long way to go before I'm The Fonz," he said.

"Not as far as you think," Ralph told him. "This collar has starch in it!"

In the ring, Pop Mauler was motioning to the crowd, asking for quiet.

"This is it, I guess," Fonzie said.

"What's your fight plan, Fonz?" Richie asked.

"I'm gonna get in there—I'm gonna get in there and—"

"Yes?"

"I'm gonna get in there and . . . and run!" Fonzie said.

Pop Mauler began addressing the spectators. "Ladies and gentlemen! The fight of the century!"

He was interrupted by a resumption of the cheering.

Fonzie climbed into the ring. While the cheering continued, Pop Mauler provided him with gloves and laced them on.

"Any special place you want the body sent?" Pop Mauler asked Fonzie.

"No, I don't want it, I don't save souvenirs," Fonzie replied. "You and Mom can take it with you when the carnival pulls out. After all, he's your son."

Pop Mauler chuckled. "Pretty fast on the comeback, aren't you?"

"If you think I'm fast on the comeback," Fonzie replied, "wait'll you see what I do with my feet."

Pop Mauler returned to the center of the ring and quieted the crowd again. "In this corner," he announced, pointing, "The Fonz!"

The crowd cheered, stomped and whistled.

"And in this corner—the Muskogee Mauler!"

The crowd booed, all except Mom Mauler. "Fry his liver, Sonny!" she shouted.

"Is that fair?" Marion asked Howard.

"That's only an expression," he explained to her.

"What she really means is 'beat his brains out' or something like that."

"Oh. Sauté his spleen!" she called out to Fonzie.

Pop Mauler summoned the fighters to the center of the ring and gave them instructions. "The same as last time—whatever I said," he told them. "And may the best man win, Sonny," he said to the Mauler. Then he sent them back to their corners.

"How do you feel, Fonz?" Richie called up. "Is the antidote working yet?"

"How can I tell with these gloves on?" Fonzie replied. "Even if I *had* a toothpick up here with me, I couldn't get hold of it."

The bell rang.

The Mauler came raging out of his corner and ran straight at Fonzie.

"It's all over but the funeral!" Mom Mauler shouted.

Fonzie ducked under the Mauler's blow and ran to the far side of the ring.

The crowd cheered.

"Is it over?" Marion asked Howard.

"This is just the first round."

"But the Mauler had his chance and missed," Marion protested. "Do you mean he gets to try again?"

"Again and again and again," Howard told her.

"Run, Arthur, run!" Marion cried out.

Fonzie was doing just that. Keeping a few steps ahead of the Mauler, he was dashing from corner to corner. The spectators, puzzled, had become quiet again.

"How many minutes?" Fonzie called down to Richie, passing his corner.

"Two more to go!"

A few boos came from the spectators.

"I think they've gotten to like the Mauler a little more," Marion said to Howard. "They're not as antagonistic toward him as they were before."

"Marion, they're not booing the Mauler now. They're booing Fonzie. They want him to fight, not run."

"Someone ought to explain to them that Fonzie has lost his strength," Marion said. "They're being very unfair! Howard—tell them!"

"Marion, I can't stand up in the middle of a fight and—"

The spectators were suddenly cheering again.

In the ring, Fonzie had halted.

"He's got his strength back!" Richie shouted excitedly.

But Fonzie was now bending down.

"He's tying his shoelace!" Howard groaned. "His shoelace is untied! He's tying his shoelace!"

The Mauler had caught up with Fonzie.

"No, he isn't!" Richie said. "He can't! He can't tie the shoelace with those gloves on!"

The Mauler swung a fist as if it were a golf club. The blow breezed by the top of Fonzie's head.

"Tee him up again!" Mom Mauler shouted.

But the swing had carried the Mauler off balance and by the time he got his bearings, Fonzie was off and running again. Once more, the crowd began booing.

"How much longer?" Fonzie asked, passing his corner.

"Thirty seconds!"

Distracted, Fonzie failed to make the next turn. He

hit the ropes and bounced back, crashing into the Mauler. The Mauler, surprised, went down, with Fonzie on top of him. There was a scramble as they both tried to rise. Pop Mauler rushed to them and tried to separate them—by standing on one of Fonzie's gloves and pulling on the Mauler.

"Kick 'im, Pop!" Mom Mauler cried out. "Remember—you're family!"

Pop Mauler kicked—and missed. The force of the kick upended him and he landed on the Mauler, flattening him. No longer held down by Pop Mauler's foot, Fonzie was able to rise.

"Bell!" Pop Mauler shouted.

By coincidence, the bell rang.

Fonzie strolled toward his corner, where Richie, Potsie and Ralph, his handlers, were waiting.

"You're winning, Fonz!" Ralph told him.

"How can I be winning?" Fonzie asked, sitting down on his stool. "How can anybody be winning? Nobody has hit anybody yet."

"Oh, is it still a fight?" Ralph said. "I thought it had been changed to a hundred-yard dash."

Richie dabbed at Fonzie's face with a towel. "Do you feel any stronger yet?" he asked.

"For this fight, that's not the right question," Fonzie replied. "You ought to be over there in the other corner, asking the Mauler if he feels any weaker yet. My strategy is to wear him out so he can't chase me any more."

The bell rang for the second round.

The Mauler was halfway across the ring, charging, by the time Fonzie rose from his stool.

"Hey, you're repeating yourself—this is how the first round started," Fonzie said, ducking.

The blow missed.

"Come on, let's go," Fonzie said, motioning to the Mauler and setting out on the circuit of the ring. "I don't like to run alone."

The Mauler trudged after him. And again the booing began.

"Fonz, not so fast," Richie called out, as Fonzie passed the corner for the dozenth time a while later. "The Mauler can't keep up!"

"I *can't* slow down!" Fonzie answered. "Something's happening!"

"He's getting his strength back!" Potsie said, as Fonzie ran on.

"Look—he's passing the Mauler!" Ralph said.

"Poor Mr. Mauler," Marion said. "He looks exhausted! Why doesn't he stop and rest for a while?"

Fonzie was running toward his corner again. "I think I got it!" he called out.

"Then stop running!" Richie shouted.

"I got to test it!" Fonzie answered. He halted and drew back a glove, then pounded it into a ringpost. The post split. "Yeah, I think I got it," Fonzie said. He turned around to face the Mauler.

The Mauler, making a turn, saw that Fonzie had stopped. He launched a charge. But he was so weary that the best he could do was fall forward.

"I can't hit a guy that would be down already anyway if he didn't have the momentum going for him," Fonzie said. He raised a glove. "Stop!"

The Mauler, unable to check his lunge, stumbled straight into the glove with his chin.

"Some guys you just can't help," Fonzie grumbled.

The Mauler dropped.

The crowd cheered.

The Mauler lay still, out cold.

Pop Mauler came sauntering up. "One," he said, starting the count. "About time for that bell," he commented to Fonzie.

"If I hear that bell," Fonzie told him, "you are going to be doing the counting from the canvas."

"I guess, on second thought, it isn't time for the bell," Pop Mauler decided. "Two," he said, resuming the count. "Two-and-one-sixteenth. Two-and-one-eighth. Two-and—one—quarter. Two—and—"

Fonzie pulled back a gloved fist.

Threefourfivesixseveneightnineten!" Pop Mauler said. He raised Fonzie's arm in victory. "The winnah! —dad-drat-it!"

The spectators went wild, swarming into the ring to collect on their bets. Fonzie had to drag the Mauler out of the way to keep him from being trampled. "Hey, Mom! Come and get your baby!" he shouted.

From somewhere out of the crowd came Mom's voice. "Throw that loser a fish!" she answered. "I had a half-buck bet on the other guy!"

Sadly, Fonzie pulled the Mauler to the safety of a neutral corner. "It's enough to make a guy stop sending Mothers' Day cards," he said. The Mauler began regaining consciousness. "No hard feelings," Fonzie said. "And to prove it," he added, leaving, "I hope you become an orphan."

When Fonzie jumped down from the ring the Cunninghams and Ralph and Potsie were waiting to congratulate him.

"Don't forget to get your purse," Howard reminded him.

"Later, after the crowd thins out," Fonzie said.

"Fonz, what happened!" Ralph said. "I didn't even see that guy touch you!"

"What're you talking about?" Fonzie asked.

"You must be punchdrunk if you're going to start carrying a purse," Ralph said.

"The winner's purse, Tweedle-dumb-dumb!"

"Oh, *that* purse."

"Well, you're The Fonz again," Howard said. "I guess that calls for a celebration. The cotton candy is on me!"

"Oh, Howard, I hope not," Marion said. "It's so sticky!"

"I mean I'm buying. After all, this has been a pretty successful day financially. I had a bet on Fonzie, remember."

"Yeah, with that bet you made," Fonzie said, as they left the Mauler's tent, "you could buy cotton candy for the whole town—if the whole town happened to be out of town."

"Look!" Marion said.

All around them, as they stepped out onto the midway, rides were being dismantled.

"Yeah, the carnival is folding its tents," Fonzie said. "And if JoJo hadn't delivered that antidote, the Maulers would now be stealing away into the night with those bets." He looked around. "I wonder where— Heyyyyyy! Here he comes!" he said, as JoJo approached, carrying a suitcase.

"Where to?" Howard asked JoJo. "Where does the carnival go from here?"

"I'm not going with the carnival," JoJo answered. He smiled. "Do you see anything different about me?"

Fonzie studied him closely. "Your collar! You're not wearing your collar!"

JoJo nodded. "I'm free," he said. "I'm leaving the carnival. I'm going to be a sculptor. Or, at least, I hope that's what I'm going to be. There's one thing I'm sure of: I'm not ever going to be JoJo the Dog-faced Boy again."

"That didn't fit you, anyway," Ralph said. "How about SamSam the Dog—"

JoJo looked at him threateningly. "My name is Joe, period," he said.

"Joe Period! That's a great name!" Ralph said.

"So, you're finally going to do it," Fonzie said to Joe.

"Thanks to you," Joe replied. "You trusted me, Fonzie, you had faith in me. You had enough faith in me to go into the ring with the Mauler. I told you that you would get your strength back and you believed me. I figure that ... well, if you could have faith in me, I ought to have some faith in myself."

"Yeah, well, you can't go wrong doing what The Fonz tells you to do," Fonzie said. "That's one of those great unwritten truths that you read about all the time."

"So long," Joe said, heading toward the exit. "I'll send you a sculpture some day."

"Yeah, make it something I can understand," Fonzie called after him. "Whittle me a piston or a carburetor!"

"Now, for that cotton candy!" Howard said.

"Hey, listen, I'm gonna skip the cotton candy," Fonzie said.

"But the celebration is in your honor," Joanie protested.

"Yeah, well, I'm gonna celebrate," Fonzie said.

"And I'm gonna celebrate with some sweets, too. Only, not cotton candy."

"I don't understand, Fonz," Howard said.

"Remember when this carnival pulled in?" Fonzie replied. "I had the hoochie-coochie dancers all dated up. Only I got sidetracked with that Lola. Now," he said, "the carnival is pulling out. And I got a lot of missed hoochie-coochie dancers to make up for."

"How do you plan to do that?" Howard asked.

"Don't ask for details," Fonzie replied. "The details are the secret recipe that makes me The Fonz."

"No, what I mean is, the carnival is leaving," Howard said. "And you know how fast these roustabouts work. An hour from now, this will be an empty lot."

"Yeah, an hour, that's about the time I need," Fonzie said. He saluted. "Enjoy your cotton candy," he said, setting out toward the Isles of Paradise, "and I'll do the same."

"In an hour!" Potsie said, watching Fonzie depart. *"All those hoochie-coochie dancers?"*

"Well, don't forget . . . he *is* The Fonz," Richie said.

"Right—there's a lot in a name," Ralph said. "That's why I suggested SamSam. Joe Period is a terrible name for a dog."

FILMS & TV

0352   Star

30006X	**THE MAKING OF KING KONG** B. Bahrenburg	60p*
398957	**THE MARRIAGE RING ("COUPLES")** Paddy Kitchen & Dulan Barber	60p
397276	**MURDER BY DEATH** H. R. F. Keating	60p*
398825	**McCOY: THE BIG RIP-OFF** Sam Stewart	50p*
398035	**PAUL NEWMAN** Michael Kerbel	75p
397470	**ODE TO BILLY JOE** Herman Raucher	60p*
398191	**THE ROCKFORD FILES** Mike Jahn	50p*
397373	**THE SCARLET BUCCANEER** D. R. Benson	60p*
398442	**THE SIX MILLION DOLLAR MAN 3: THE RESCUE OF ATHENA ONE** Mike Jahn	45p*
398647	**THE SIX MILLION DOLLAR MAN 4: PILOT ERROR** Jay Barbree	50p*
396490	**SIX MILLION DOLLAR MAN 5: THE SECRET OF BIGFOOT** Mike Jahn	60p
396852	**SPACE 1999: (No. 2) MIND BREAKS OF SPACE** Michael Butterworth	60p
396660	**SPACE 1999 (No. 1) PLANETS OF PERIL** Michael Butterworth	60p
398531	**SPANISH FLY** Madelaine Duke	50p
398817	**SWITCH** Mike Jahn	50p*
398051	**THE ULTIMATE WARRIOR** Bill S. Ballinger	50p*

0426   Tandem

180240	**AT THE EARTH'S CORE** Edgar Rice Burroughs	50p
180321	**THE LAND THAT TIME FORGOT** Edgar Rice Burroughs	50p
164164	**LENNY** Valerie Kohler Smith	50p*
16184X	**ONEDIN LINE: THE HIGH SEAS** Cyril Abraham	60p
132661	**ONEDIN LINE: THE IRON SHIPS**	60p
168542	**SHAMPOO** Robert Alley	50p

*Not for sale in Canada.

0352   Star

396391	A STAR IS BORN Alexander Edwards	60p
396792	THE BIONIC WOMAN (No. 1) DOUBLE IDENTITY Maud Willis	50p*
39689X	BIONIC WOMAN (No. 2) A QUESTION OF LIFE	50p*
396175	THE BLACK BIRD Alexander Edwards	45p*
398256	CANNON: THE FALLING BLONDE Paul Denver	50p*
396728	CANNON: IT'S LONELY ON THE SIDEWALK	50p*
396687	CARQUAKE Michael Avallone	60p
397349	COLUMBO: ANY OLD PORT IN A STORM Henry Clement	50p*
398183	COLUMBO: A CHRISTMAS KILLING Alfred Lawrence	45p*
300795	COLUMBO: THE DEAN'S DEATH	40p*
30099X	DIRTY HARRY Phillip Roch	60p
396903	EMMERDALE FARM (No. 1) THE LEGACY Lee Mackenzie	50p
396296	EMMERDALE FARM: (No. 2) PRODIGAL'S PROGRESS Lee Mackenzie	60p
397489	ESCAPE FROM THE DARK Rosemary Anne Sisson	50p
398744	GABLE AND LOMBARD Joe Morella & Edward Z. Epstein	60p*
397160	HARRY & WALTER GO TO NEW YORK Sam Stewart	50p*
398493	HAWAII 5-0: THE ANGRY BATTALION Herbert Harris	50p*
300876	HAWAII 5-0: SERPENTS IN PARADISE	45p*
396288	HEAVEN HAS NO FAVOURITES Erich Maria Remarque	75p
398477	HUSTLE Stephen Shagan	60p*
398574	INNOCENTS WITH DIRTY HANDS Richard Neely	60p*
397500	INSERTS Anton Rimart	60p
397438	KOJAK: GIRL IN THE RIVER Victor B. Miller	50p*
397357	KOJAK: GUN BUSINESS	50p*
397446	KOJAK: MARKED FOR MURDER	50p*
398671	KOJAK: TAKE-OVER	50p*

*Not for sale in Canada.

0352 Star

General (all are illustrated)

396885	Margaret Duchess of Argyl **FORGET NOT**	70p
399078	The Duchess of Bedford **NICOLE NOBODY**	75p
300485	Helen Cathcart **ANNE AND THE PRINCESSES ROYAL**	75p
397004	Tommy Cooper **JUST LIKE THAT!**	50p
39854X	Paul Dunn **THE OSMONDS**	80p*
397071	Margot Fonteyn **MARGOT FONTEYN**	75p
396901	Gerold Frank **JUDY** (Large Format)	£1.95p
300299	Noele Gordon **MY LIFE AT CROSSROADS**	50p
396108	Brian Johnston **IT'S BEEN A LOT OF FUN**	60p
396873	Renee Jordan **STREISAND**	75p
39844X	Hildegarde Knef **THE VERDICT**	95p
398841	Vera Lynn **VOCAL REFRAIN**	60p
300973	Ralph Martin **THE STORY OF THE DUKE AND DUCHESS OF WINDSOR. THE WOMAN HE LOVED**	95p*
397039	Jessie Matthews **OVER MY SHOULDER**	60p
398396	Pat Phoenix **ALL MY BURNING BRIDGES**	60p
397578	Raymond **RAYMOND**	75p
396806	Brian Rix **MY FARCE FROM MY ELBOW**	75p
397497	John Stonehouse **JOHN STONEHOUSE – MY TRIAL**	95p
396876	Charles Thompson **BING**	70p
398384	Peter Underwood **DANNY LA RUE: LIFE'S A DRAG**	55p
397288	Mike and Bernie Winters **SHAKE A PAGODA TREE**	60p
398302	Mike Yarwood **AND THIS IS ME!**	50p
300098	**ERIC AND ERNIE: THE AUTOBIOGRAPHY OF MORECAMBE & WISE**	50p

*Not for sale in Canada.

Wyndham Books are obtainable from many booksellers and newsagents. If you have any difficulty please send purchase price plus postage on the scale below to:

Wyndham Cash Sales,
44 Hill Street
London W1X 8LB

While every effort is made to keep prices low, it is sometimes necessary to increase prices at short notice. Wyndham Books reserve the right to show new retail prices on covers which may differ from those advertised in the text or elsewhere.

Postage and Packing Rate
U.K. & Eire
One book 15p plus 7p per copy for each additional book ordered to a maximum charge of 57p.

These charges are subject to Post Office charge fluctuations.